LAST ACTS

A NOVEL

ALEXANDER SAMMARTINO

SCRIBNER

NEW YORK   LONDON   TORONTO   SYDNEY   NEW DELHI

Scribner
An Imprint of Simon & Schuster, Inc.
1230 Avenue of the Americas
New York, NY 10020

First Scribner hardcover edition January 2024

SCRIBNER and design are registered trademarks of The Gale Group, Inc., used under license by Simon & Schuster, Inc., the publisher of this work.

Simon & Schuster: Celebrating 100 Years of Publishing in 2024

For information about special discounts for bulk purchases, please contact Simon & Schuster Special Sales at 1-866-506-1949 or business@simonandschuster.com.

The Simon & Schuster Speakers Bureau can bring authors to your live event. For more information or to book an event, contact the Simon & Schuster Speakers Bureau at 1-866-248-3049 or visit our website at www.simonspeakers.com.

Interior design by Hope Herr-Cardillo

Manufactured in the United States of America

10 9 8 7 6 5 4 3 2 1

Library of Congress Cataloging-in-Publication Data has been applied for.

ISBN 978-1-9821-9674-5
ISBN 978-1-9821-9675-2 (ebook)

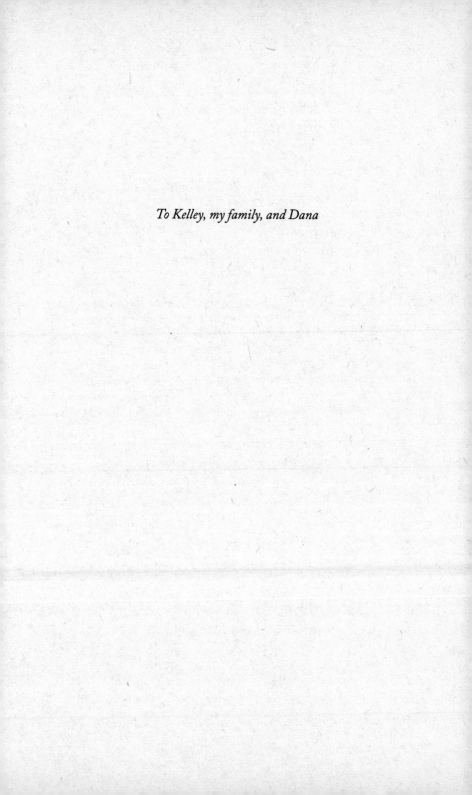

To Kelley, my family, and Dana

Man errs. Man does not merely stray into errancy. He is always astray in errancy . . .

—Martin Heidegger

I

2014

1

Saved, yes. David Rizzo knew his son's resurrection had saved his gun shop. The arrival of this fact—abrupt, vivid—brought him to silent tears behind the wheel of his unreliable Eldorado. He drove through the depthless desert sky, wiping his face, the world a smear of bare earth and sunlight. Rizzo's Firearms, rescued. His son, not dead. It settled between his stomach and his throat, this stark revelation.

As Rizzo drove to the hospital on that heat-sick afternoon to pick up his son—drove fast across the tall loop of the freeway, over the lifeless suburbs: Sonora Gateway, Arroyo Foothills, Moon Valley Manors; above the carnival spreads of outdoor shopping centers: Desert Ridge, Scottsdale Quarter, Metrocenter; past the pockets of turf fields, car dealerships, adobe churches, drive-through liquor stores, uncharmed apartments; as he drove on beside the midday glitter of the casino, Talking Stick, across boundless land streaked with posing saguaros, then the barbed purple columns of the east valley mountains, Superstition, toward the minor glass of downtown—yes, as Rizzo drove through his home of Phoenix, Arizona, he began to unbend all the angles of his elaborate salvation.

All his life he had waited for a sign from above. Here it was, his estranged son, back for a reason. It had been more than a year since he had last seen the kid. And of all days this one: when Rizzo was supposed to sign the shop away, the call came. Overdosed three days ago, he said. Flatlined. Nicholas, on the phone with that familiar mumble, meek and sorry. It was obvious: if his son could return from the dead, so could

Rizzo's business. Now, in the clay-colored valley of the desert, all was glory, all was light, all burned with the eternal grace of the divine.

The Eldorado's engine was smoking. Rizzo, distressed, parked in what seemed like the only open spot at Banner Health. His shit engine. Outside the car he paced around, afraid the whole thing might catch fire. Seared the shit out of his fingers when he tried to lift the hood. He twisted his pinkie ring, patted the gray curls at the back of his head, hoping the coils of smoke would suddenly quit. They did not.

After walking a mile to the Circle K for some coolant—a lonelier journey than Rizzo anticipated: he leaned through the dust knocked into the air, the one man on the roadside, and the sound of every truck bed rattling past made him feel as if he was somehow left behind—Rizzo got back to the hospital just in time to watch his Eldorado be loaded onto a tow truck. How could he have missed the sign that said those spots were reserved for medical vehicles? Rizzo, dumbstruck, sweated through his silk shirt, still hugging the container of coolant, unsure of how to spare his Cadillac the sad ordeal of the tow yard.

"You see that last night? Six dead. Fourteen injured. Sorority girls, deputies, cyclists," the tow truck guy said, tearing several identical pieces of paper from a clipboard. He was a man of frail build and dense beard. "Makes you wonder. Some maniac in a car, mind gone, shooting everyone. You never know. Right here right now. Could be us. Except this kid hated women or something and wanted to kill them all. But hey, you never know. We could be women. It could've been us. Random, everything, right?"

The tow truck guy socially pondering a recent massacre meant the vehicle was safe—or so Rizzo thought, but then a button was pressed and the car rose with a groan to the flatbed.

Of course this was not a big deal. In the grand scheme. Calmly Rizzo, inside the hospital, introduced himself to the first-floor receptionist, who sent him to the second-floor receptionist, who held up a finger while she called the first-floor receptionist before unloading Rizzo on Maria, a lisping medical assistant who, phone pinned between shoulder and ear, steered a stretcher through the packed hall.

"Unforgivable. Totally unforgivable," Maria said to her phone.

Rizzo jogged beside her, explaining. His son? Yes, his son, you know: Nick Rizzo—the tall kid with the crazy hair who might be decent-looking if he put some weight on—brought in because of an overdose?

But Maria did not know. So Rizzo repeated all he knew, how he had been trying to reach his son on the number the kid had called from but got only a busy signal. In response a laconic Maria said to take the elevator to the third floor and walk to the east wing, two lefts, a quick right, and Rizzo said he planned to do just that, but he first wanted to talk to the doctor. The old guy spread on the stretcher pointed a finger at Rizzo. "Do me a favor, please. Hey. Okay? A favor." He was a wrinkled man with striking eyebrows. "Tell Charlie Miniscus I hope he rots in hell."

Everything stayed in motion: Maria with her stretcher, but also a flurry of creaking wheelchairs, wobbling gowns, a traffic of the diseased and the damned—and there went Rizzo, weaving to keep up, embarrassed and breathless.

"The doctors are in meetings," Maria said, walking faster now. All of them? "One second," Maria said, to her phone, while looking at Rizzo. She said she understood now, and then repeated her earlier directions: third floor, two lefts, a quick right. The guy on the stretcher again: "Rot in hell, Miniscus!"

Rizzo smiled at everyone in the elevator so that they all understood how completely fine he was. Oh, he was so fine. A sallow man in the corner of the compartment wept, Rizzo noticed, while incanting the word *kidney*.

Maria's directions brought Rizzo to a florid man in a suit who, with his legs crossed in a wheelchair parked near a bathroom, stood to introduce himself. "Chad Garlin. Hey there, how you doing?" Chad—who was just fantastic, thanks for asking—happened to be a medical supplies salesman from AventCore specializing in heavy-duty gauze. "Best stuff for your gunshot wounds, your buzz-saw wounds, any impaling situations." And he was on break, technically, Chad choosing this wheelchair here because he spent much of his day walking up and down the stairs for his meetings with doctors. "Good way to get my steps in," Chad continued. Up, down. Up, down. Half his day, lost in the dumb metal heat of the stairwell. How many steps had Rizzo taken today, Chad wanted to know. How many? Chad mimicked a marching motion. It amazed him how doctors could be so oblivious when it came to their own health, he said, slapping Rizzo's shoulder. "Oh, is that right, not a doctor?" Chad, dimming, lowered himself back into the wheelchair, then directed Rizzo with a wave toward a far window.

Rizzo found the area disastrously hot, the hallway a blur, and the only person around was the janitor, a confident man with a limp, mopping, who explained they had moved all the patients in the third-floor east wing to the first-floor west wing because of the busted AC. "Or at least that's the story they're telling," the janitor whispered. After listening to the janitor's theory—basic experiments: risky organ removals, unproven pharmaceuticals—Rizzo was back in the first-floor west wing, near where he had entered, and soon he figured out from a cafeteria worker with an eyebrow piercing that his son was no longer in the hospital; that is, his son had been sent across the street to the health system's psychiatric center, the place they used for the detox spillover.

Not that any of this frustrated Rizzo. Oh no, not one bit. It all almost made sense.

Rizzo halted and sprinted in accordance with the traffic on his way to retrieve his son. After a day in a coma, after three days of detox, Nick looked even worse than Rizzo expected: pale, sunken, forlorn. He had a lazy beard and the curls in his hair were greased to the right side of his head. Nicholas Rizzo, his stupid fragile son. He stood there in the lobby waiting, glum and unkempt, in jeans and a flannel. Behind the front desk a man said, "And in my opinion he got what he deserved," into his headphones. Rizzo gave his son a firm nod that he hoped communicated what a shit time this would be to talk.

Outside they waited for an Uber in silence. It was at this point that Rizzo realized he was still holding the container of coolant. The car that came was a minivan, and the driver apologized about all the stuff they needed to climb over: dented boxes of TiVos, iPods, DVDs, smart alarm clocks, noisy baby toys. The driver was helping a friend unload some stuff—speaking of which, the driver said, a thumb over his shoulder, if they saw anything they liked? Let him know. He could maybe possibly perhaps make a deal. So just let him know, okay?

They sat crammed in the last row. "My phone," Nick whispered, all the sudden. A frantic pat down followed. "Shit." Leaning back, dejected. Then, hands behind his head: "Hey, Dad? Thanks for coming. I'm sorry about all of this. But things are different this time, I don't need rehab. The hospital was enough."

In a rare occurrence, Rizzo agreed. This rehab crap? Not worth it. Same with NA. For some it helped, but for others, like you, my son, all it does is acquaint idiots with more accomplished idiots. So instead of rehab Nick would work—as in, work for his father's business.

"Oh." Nick, scratching his head. "Wait. You're still doing the gun thing?"

It would be easy to sleep tonight, Rizzo knew, because there was absolutely nothing to worry about. Rizzo was okay. He was at the kitchen table with a cigarette. This was a good table, a scarce heirloom, the surface tiles painted by his own grandmother, the place where many a Rizzo had graced a meal with a pile of complaints. He looked around the house. The desert landscape paintings of uncertain origin. The little crucifix hung beside a wrought-iron star. Envelopes stacked on the counter beneath a cordless landline. Rizzo now began to feel these objects no longer belonged to him but rather to the house itself, this collapsed version of a home with its low ceiling and an open kitchen and a single hallway, a structure identical to those owned by neighbors he had never spoken to nor seen but whom he knew existed by the infrequent grating lift from their garage doors. He was the rare year-round resident in a community of second homes. Rizzo ashed his cigarette in a plain mug his wife for some reason had liked, staring through the dust-streaked glass of the slider door at the yard of decorative rock.

It would make sense to worry if he had no plan. His thirty-year-old son, back again, marooned in the house, and no plan? His business, his stupendous debt, and no plan? But there was no need to worry because he knew he would come up with something, a way to save his gun shop, his son, himself. There was no need to worry because, the last time Rizzo checked, this was still America, and in America there would always be hope.

2

So then why was Rizzo crying?

Why?

Mere hours after he had been so certain, and yet here he was outside, as far away as he could be from his son—who sat like an idiot at the kitchen island, hauling cereal to his face—in a corner of his backyard, poorly obscured by the drooping mesquite, crying?

Crying, in what was officially the palm tree twilight?

Beneath the mountains streaked in a brittle green? In a backyard so new, so ready for use, with fake flagstone, a propane grill, and heat-cracked wicker chairs? Why?

Who cries in paradise?

3

Here were the qualities that made him Rizzo.

He owned an accomplished vocabulary of gestures. Most common were the single fist shake and the double finger twirl. These gave him access to a needed realm of emphasis: the fist shake might stress the force of his blissful exaltation, the twirl could signal a note of deep irony in otherwise monotone despair. He held convoluted grievances, all of which were expressed with his palms held toward his audience. Mid-monologue, he pointed in apparently arbitrary directions to establish his separation from the source of his outrage. He was often outraged. He was also often elated, a fact that took the form of his hands pressing together and swinging forth as if in anointment. He was a man of nods and winks and eyebrow raises. He pinched his fingers. He tapped his temple. He swept an honest arm through the air. His most frequent expression? The silent squint, a look both concerned and confused. He bit his bottom lip while he walked—a custom of the nervous dreamer. For Rizzo these were no less instinctive than the kick that followed a strike to the knee.

His outfits had dulled from years of consistent wear. He wore clothes that belonged to destinations. Denim shirts, tropical button-downs. His rings, his bracelet, his watch—all seemed foreign to the times. In the mirror, he got the sense he had misplaced some part of himself yet could not identify the name of what he had lost. Nothing fit right. Age had come upon him. He still liked above all to laugh, but he no longer liked the sound of his laugh. He found himself touching the front of his skull, amazed at the reality of his scalp. "I'm sorry," he seemed to be saying, everywhere. At gatherings he was fated to end up alone near the trash cans. He could be seen paused in a parking lot, cigarette in mouth, squinting over his shoulder at the bottom of a defeated loafer. He believed a man was the sum of his actions, and he was dismayed by his own total.

Luckily there was still television. His show of the moment was *I Survived a Crime*. Last week there were back-to-back episodes featuring surveillance footage from shootings, stabbings, and brawls in subway mezzanines. It was far more than the spectacle of the violence that captivated Rizzo, it was the proof that humans might outlast such violence. He never missed an airing of *Rescue Cam*. He watched shows where specious experts were resolved to save hoarders, restaurants, bars—none of which, Rizzo soon noticed, ever deserved to be saved. Appealing to summer paranoia, hours of episodes lauded shark attacks. He had completed multiple marathons of *Nature Gone Wild*. Never had he thought he might witness a black bear tackle a human being. The power! The terror.

Between his shows Rizzo watched the commercial breaks with equal fascination. An ad for Subaru showed a delighted family on a late-night drive smashed off the road by a semitruck. An ad for Nike featured interviews with triathletes who had all lost spouses to colon cancer. In the ad for Vasotec, the leading medication for heart failure, a chef dicing scallions stopped to seize the chest of his apron, twirl, and then collapse on the floor of a commercial kitchen. From where had all of this death arrived? In the year Rizzo and his son had been separated, it seemed to appear everywhere. He thought he might conjure a stroke just at the repetition of the word. Oh, it was death! It was death.

Still, as a guy who had stumbled beyond his prime, television was Rizzo's redeemer. All he had been taught from the box! How to live, how to fight, how to love. Far from the same with his phone. His phone made him available, vulnerable, always. His phone exposed him to the fraught depths of his unknowing. It terrified him, to hold his vibrating screen while on the glass there appeared an unfamiliar number. He feared the purpose of every call was to bring news of some shattering disaster. The phone reminded him that he was himself, forever caught in uncertainty—but in front of the television he was joyfully absorbed.

Rizzo had a way to watch, a pose he had mastered through the decades of striving to forget the losses of the day. On his leather sofa, reclined, extended, with his ankles crossed, with his hands folded over his torso—here he merged with the material of the couch and the particles of light from the screen, glowing. This was how he often found himself, in the creaking hours after midnight, when he woke to a shrieking infomercial, startled by the slashed price.

And it was to this position on the couch that Rizzo brought himself after he finished crying alone in the yard. He was aware of, and annoyed by, his son at the kitchen island. His shirtless child, still spooning milk from his cereal bowl. He had thought this scrawny homeless bum could help?

"Don't you want something besides cereal?" Rizzo spoke to the back of his son. "I've got bread. I've got provolone. Turkey, salami, whatever you want. What's wrong with sandwiches?"

Silence. Nick stared into his bowl. The depressing prominence of Nick's ribs, the skinny downcast frame—the disregard Nick showed toward his body suddenly seemed to Rizzo like an attack on his father.

Rizzo, louder: "I can always grill. I can grill in the dark. Burgers, sausages. What, now you're some crazy Buddhist who only eats seaweed?"

A silence now malicious. Before Rizzo could unload a more pointed series of questions about when his son became such an ungrateful little shit, Nick got up from his chair, mumbled something about a headache, then shuffled down the hall, gone.

Every time Rizzo opened his mouth he remembered why it had been closed. He remained in his spot on the couch, discouraged with himself, while the local news told of a ten-car freeway crash, a suburban pool drowning, a playground shooting, multiple bobcat attacks, twice as many ICE raids—it was unclear if the events occurred in that order—and a conclusive visit to the butterfly wonderland. Then came an ad for Friar Lighting in which a man wearing an orange cowl and turquoise crucifix described the endless watts in his lighting warehouse—"Go toward the light!"—while in the background an Aerosmith-indebted song played: "Beam On."

The man in the ad was Bill Friar, owner, actor, winner. It was not the ad itself that Rizzo had an issue with—it was the bullshit optimism that made Bill Friar think his business worthy of an advertisement. Go fuck yourself, Bill! It was the same with all of the valley businessmen who stormed through the local television channels with their ads for weekend deals. Rizzo hated them, he wished he was one of them. They were all idiots. They were also all rich. Take Bill Bingo, of Bingo Real Estate, with his thirty-second ads of dumb luxury. Mustached Bill, in a brown felt cowboy hat, in front of some Paradise Valley mansion. It was the same with Nate Straight, owner of Chandler's No Bull Ford. Nate was a giant specimen whose confidence fit his pro ball frame. In his ad Nate dressed up as a matador, swung around a muleta and stabbed the air with a floppy sword while vehicles burst on the lot. A ridiculous achievement was still an achievement: the man owned a helicopter, which featured in another ad. Salon Suzie's newest showed a montage of her prior ads before zooming out to her in front of a green screen where she told viewers that everyone who booked their next appointment through her website would be entered into a raffle to direct their very own Salon Suzie ad. She stood there smiling with the cheery persistence of a psychopath.

Rizzo knew he did not have it, the self-certainty that these other owners showed. It was a sense of being chosen. They willed their worlds. He spilled his disasters. After his salesmanship, he was confident most in his inabilities. It had worsened ever since his son disappeared, the insecurity. What had he done? His son's absence had to be his fault. He had left his door unlocked all year in case Nick lost his key but wanted to come home.

Rizzo left the couch and walked down the hall until he stood, in silence, in front of Nick's door.

"Nick?" Rizzo called. "Nick!"

"What?" The voice of his son.

Rizzo, in the hall: "Just wanted to see if you need anything before bed," before listing the things he thought his son might need before bed: toothbrush, toothpaste, alcohol-free mouthwash, heavy-duty dental floss, a glass of water, some juice—plenty of orange juice in the house, and you like pulp-free, right, Nick?—yeah, glasses of water and orange juice and also a couple granola bars in case Nick woke up and felt—

"Are you okay?" This was his son's question. "You're, like, yelling."

"Me? Okay?" Which, lowering his hands from above his head, Rizzo heard as louder than he intended. "How about a simple thank-you for a father who goes out of his way to make sure you have snacks? How many recovering drug addicts have snacks?" He waited for a response, got none, slouched back to his spot beneath the TV.

4

On the kitchen table: cigarette packs, mugs, ashtrays, and mugs that had become ashtrays. Sunlight through the window above the sink. Early morning. The beige wall held a teal clock, formal portraits of relatives, and a cheap winter landscape painting with snow landing on horses in a corral. There was an unexpected charm to the clutter in the light.

Nick, shirtless, moved his spoon around his bowl. Rizzo stared at Nick while battering his eggs with pepper, a process that shook his crucifix necklace. Shirtless himself, he felt like the husky double of his son. He dumped sugar in his coffee, then overcame his eggs in a few bites. After looking over his chest and stomach, Rizzo grabbed a cigarette from a stray pack. He sat there, smoking, looking past his child.

It was not until his wife left that Rizzo learned there were people who preferred not to yell. Sometimes he still forgot. It was how he made his point, the volume. Why else would he shout? He was in love.

He needed to be sure this understanding was shared by his son. "Hey, Nick," Rizzo said, sending smoke through his nose. "When we were talking last night, I—"

"What?" Nick, chewing, searched the packs for a cigarette of his own.

"Last night, I said. When we were talking. I didn't mean to yell at you."

"Okay."

"Okay?"

"I'm going back to bed." Nick held up a pack, found nothing inside, picked up another. "Every time I would start to drift off I would reach over to set an alarm, then panic because I couldn't find my phone. The Suboxone makes me tired but it's not enough to knock me out."

"Well, it's probably for the best," Rizzo said.

"Not really. Couldn't sleep at all in the hospital either. Shivered until I puked most nights. Then there was this guy next to me screaming because he couldn't figure out how to tie a strong enough knot with his bed sheets to hang himself."

"I meant the phone, Nick," jabbing the plate with his cigarette. Rizzo lit another, then slid the pack and lighter across the table to Nick. They were silent, smoking. Rizzo next spoke without looking up from his plate. "Found a rehab out in Casa Grande that seems reasonable."

"Oh."

"Only place that doesn't make you pay the full upfront. You do a deposit, right, then you pay the remainder at the end."

"That seems fair."

"It shouldn't have to be upfront. I should be able to see how it goes. I should have an opportunity for assessment." It felt urgent to Rizzo to say this.

Nick, smoke coming out of his mouth: "Casa Grande." Then: "What happened to me working for you?"

As he left the table, Rizzo said: "I came back down to planet Earth."

5

Off the 101 and Cave Creek Road, mountains looming, was where you would find Rizzo's Firearms. Which was not to say it was an easy find. An unpainted strip of asphalt broke without warning off the main road to wind through a commercial wasteland. There were no signs. There were mounds of toppled chain-link, scrap heaps, unleased strip malls. For this reason the area appealed most to drivers who wanted to spend a few hours undetected: those who were eager to drug themselves dumb or there to inspect the pyramids of discarded objects scattered about. Starved coyotes trotted alone through the shining dust, sniffing at piles of worn tires. The constant sun made time seem stuck. A purplish wall, dividing the road from the bridge of freeway, was macadamized with white and yellow and green rock to resemble a thirty-foot-long lizard, but the tar binding the rock, worn from years of brutal sunlight, had begun to fade—as had the colors of the rocks—so that the lizard was now little more than a grave industrial stain.

This nameless road intersected with a few short streets, along which there were occasionally businesses still in operation. For instance: Global Turf, a warehouse committed to the manufacture of artificial grass composed with the recycled rubber from shredded tractor tires. And One-Stop Restaurant, a local depot that stored torso-sized quantities of condiments and boasted a limitless supply of lobster. Ralph's Junkyard, the business closest to Twenty-sixth Street, had a broken magnetic crane stalled high above corroded cliffs of disposed metal. Between Ralph's and

One-Stop there was the turnoff that led to what was called, strangely, a business park, which in fact was a slightly elevated cul-de-sac with a loaf of stucco at its center, a building housing several businesses, the building where, finally, you would find Rizzo's Firearms.

Rizzo had been lured by the promise that the land behind the business park would be harrowed into a condominium farm. More than four years in, the ground out back was still unbroken. Buford Bellum, sham developer of the desert, was the one to thank. His veneers and dyed goatee were on signs announcing miles of nowhere all across the valley. It was right after the worst of the recession, maybe early '09, when Rizzo first noticed the billboards for Bellum Industries off the I-10. Buford, with his shocking tan, next to a model design of town homes. It was a plan simple enough for any idiot. Buy for cheap, wait for the recovery, create a sense of what could be, then sell high to some foreign conglomerate that had been researching consumer geographic trends.

Evidently the transmission towers made potential buyers back out, the fear being that any commercial property would be class-capped by the sight. Rizzo never minded: he liked to sit out back smoking on a lawn chair, staring at the lattices; the steel rows formed a honeycombed succession, fading, through the clean endless sky.

Too late, too late, I got there too late. That was the refrain of the loser. But somehow Rizzo managed to be too early. Imagine that. Early bird who choked on the worm.

After picking up the Cadillac from the tow yard—a process that only involved several humiliations, all of which Rizzo might have accepted as routine, but the presence of his son made each permanent and cruel and enfeebling; it began with the Uber driver, a woman in floral scrubs who, despite Rizzo's protests, detoured to a McDonald's to purchase four coffees—she was coming off a sixteen-hour shift—and then made Rizzo hold the cardboard drink carrier because she couldn't risk any coffee spilling on her seat beads, but because the lids had not been put on right, Rizzo spent the ride being burned on his hands and thighs; then there was the tow yard itself, where Rizzo tried, and failed, to negotiate the price of retrieval, a negotiation that concluded with the tow yard manager—who had a skull tattooed on each hand—saying that if Rizzo beat him in an arm-wrestling match, he could name his price; naturally Rizzo lost, but, worse, he believed he would win with enough attempts: best two out of three, then of five, then of seven, and so on, until Nick pointed out that Rizzo's knuckles had started to bleed from being smashed against the counter; Rizzo then gingerly drove the Eldorado, which was still liable to explode, to a garage, where the mechanic was a polite man with braces who said the best course of action was to junk the thing—he offered to help by removing the interior for a low rate—and this time it was Nick who spoke, saying thanks but no thanks, the pair instead settling for several gallons of water and containers of coolant.

And so, relieved from his immediate fears, Rizzo now had to argue with Nick about stopping at the gun shop. They waited for the light to change at a desolate intersection.

"I've never seen it," Nick said.

"And you won't see it," Rizzo said. "Because now is not the time."

"I also need to go to the bathroom," Nick said.

Rizzo pointed a finger at his son. "I'll let you stall. That's fine. But it won't change anything."

"All I'm saying," Nick said, "is I can't hold it for an hour."

It was noon when they got to the shop, and every parking space was open. Sunlight flashed across the building's tinted windows. No wind, no traffic sounds. Clanking from the junkyard. As soon as Rizzo got out of the car he felt the punching heat.

Rizzo's Firearms was, in essence, like any other store. There was an ornamental stack of bullet boxes beside a rack of camo gear. Tiny American flags lined the tops of the aisles. Beige carpeting reached toward a three-wall exhibit of bright firearms. From inside their glass displays, the chrome barrels of handguns gave off a cold glow. There was a sheen to the dark wood of the shotguns. Most abundant were the carbines and assault rifles, all of which resembled spines of errant vertebrae. The interior of the shop might be generously called minimal and more accurately called bland, but the presence of these weapons changed the air. Even Rizzo felt this as he made his way inside the shop each day. Yes, it was true that the gun took its form from no object in nature, but the response to the appearance of a gun could not be more instinctive: terror mixed with awe.

"Huh" was what Nick said, as he looked into a case of Glocks. He wore a flannel, shorts, socks, sandals. "Guns," he said.

"Guns," Rizzo repeated. Then: "The bathroom's right here," leading Nick to a door before the warehouse. It was an impressively little bathroom that Rizzo kept immaculate.

Nick asked if Rizzo planned to stand there watching.

"Correct," Rizzo said. He gave a finger twirl. "Let's go."

"You don't trust me?"

Silence from Rizzo. Then: "Maybe you found something in your room this morning and, well . . ."

Nick pulled out his pockets. "Search me then," he said. "See what you find."

Rizzo made Nick hold out his arms and spread his legs, not knowing what he was looking for, exactly—but he tried to act efficiently unloving. He moved his hands from shoulder to flannel wrist. He put his palms to Nick's ribs. He crouched, slid his hands around his kid, finding nothing except the frame. He felt the top of his socked feet, pressing down between the toes. So strange to touch his son. This was it? Nothing more. This sad pack of bone? Here was where all the years led: Rizzo searching his son before the bathroom. And yet this anguish could not deny Rizzo his gratitude. He was lucky. His son was here, grabbable. And as long as he could wrap his arms around the stringy neck of his son, all might be okay—he knew this like he had known nothing else in his life. It was a feeling that brought a shake to his hands. His son! Kneeling, he looked up. The poor face of his son. Veins showed in the skin beneath his eyes.

Nick, in a tone clearly pained: "Happy?"

Eyes down, Rizzo told Nick to come out back when he finished.

Rizzo walked through the warehouse, picked up the bag of cat food on his way. Shooed this afternoon from the dumpsters of One-Stop Restaurant, several calicos lounged in the thin shadows striped across the unused parking spaces, waiting for Rizzo. He had never been a cat person—he was a known allergic—but their residence had been enough to send him speeding to the pet store for kibble. In the shadowed corner where he kept their bowls several cats now weaved between his legs while others cried from their spots on the loose rock floor of the alleyway. He rubbed a knuckle against the cheek of a black cat with a single eye purring on a cinder block.

"Hey, Rizzo!" It was his friend Felicia, leaning out the back door of her shop. "You're an asshole," she said.

Unfortunate but not unexpected. He came over to Southwest Pool Stuff, apologies prepared.

Felicia tapped her back pockets for a lighter. Rizzo walked behind her to the chairs, where they took their regular spots, back pain and all. It was sunlight straight to the mountains. A few hawks sank away from the power lines.

With the appropriate corresponding gestures—in this case: aggressive pointing, several claps, a few salutes—Rizzo told Felicia what happened. He was on his way to meet Buford. He had every intent to follow through. He so much appreciated all she had done to bring them together, to make the sale possible—but then his son called. How could he think about the shop? (He omitted the part where he thought exclusively about the shop.) He was thinking about his son, he said. Could

Buford be that petty? How? How could Buford, the Concrete King of Phoenix, believe that David Rizzo had intentionally shafted him? That Rizzo's nonappearance was, even in the slightest, a go-fuck-yourself?

"You made me look stupid," she said.

And he felt bad for that. He told her so.

"You'll need to kiss Buford's ass. Big time." Felicia, deadpan: "Or you could always rob the bank. Go out big."

Rizzo, equally dry: "I don't have the confidence."

Felicia held up a boot heel, put out her cigarette, dropped the filter in a coffee can. "My cousin Billy lost his house, bounced around for a while. Now he's a Satanist. Happiest I've ever seen him."

The back door opened. There he was, Nick Rizzo, the miracle himself.

Felicia slid her sunglasses lower on her nose, looking Nick over. "How long have you been shooting dope?" she asked.

Nick stretched his arms over his head, yawned. "I'm all done," he said. "If we still have to go?"

They still had to go.

The Ensconcing Hands Treatment Center was a single-story stretch of adobe. The nearest establishment was a gas station with an adjoining car wash fifteen minutes west. Barren in all directions: rocky, green, despairing. The afternoon smelled of fresh exhaust from the cars speeding south to Tucson. A cargo train crawled along the horizon, vanishing behind the mountains.

Inside, after Rizzo listened to the intake specialist detail Ensconcing Hands's core values—candor, mercy, and spiritual indemnification—in a room with both a sink and a desktop computer; then after listening to Nick's pedantic responses to questions from the dependency evaluator in a different room that looked like it had been decorated by rabid kindergarteners; after a tour through the Social Spheres, the Treatment Spaces, and the Banquet Area, where emaciated kids wandered around with spent expressions ("How are we even, like, defining overdose? If

I wanted that much shit, then wouldn't it be the correct dose?")—yes, during the last step of intake, Initial Remittance, Rizzo's card was declined.

"Maybe it's your machine," Rizzo said. His wallet and a dozen cards were spread across the counter. He was speaking to Jeremy, a dangerously large member of the Ensconcing Hands staff who performed the movements of a chuckle without releasing any sound. "When's the last time you had this machine inspected? You're sure it's up to code?" Rizzo had his elbows on the counter now. He glanced behind him at Nick, who stared at the ground, looking tormented. Rizzo leaned closer to Jeremy, whispering. "Can I just leave him here for a few hours and then, you know, come back?"

He could not.

Father and son, in a grinding silence, drove home through the crisp foothills.

6

There were of course many reasons why Nick might walk into the backyard while Rizzo was out here smoking, and many of these had nothing to do with violence. He might have a question. Or a simple concern. He might be lonely. He might have thought of something funny. His son, unshaven, barefoot, in a pair of cotton shorts, walking across the gravel in the pinkish dusk toward Rizzo—oh, it was likely harmless. And yet what Rizzo now felt at the sight of his son could be described only as magnificent terror.

But, wait. Was Nick crying? His son? Nick Rizzo, with a hand failing to cover his twisted face, crying?

With his head sort of bobbing, shaking his stupid curls?

Had Rizzo ever seen his adult son cry?

Had Rizzo ever wanted to see his adult son cry?

Why did crying, Rizzo wondered, look so much like death? Uncontrolled expressions, entangled gestures, a grueling portrait of pain.

And what was Rizzo supposed to do now? Touch this guy? This blubbering non-child? In the heat, with the heaves, to touch this person he had no choice but to know as his son? And what if Nick noticed—how could he not?—Rizzo's hesitation to act?

7

Night through the kitchen window. The portrait of horses in silver. Ashtrays, precariously stacked on mugs, at an edge of the table. Father and son sat across from each other. Rizzo lit a cigarette. Curling smoke. He looked everywhere except at Nick. The clock in yellow from the standing lamp. So quiet that he heard his cigarette burning. Nick reached for Rizzo's pack, lit one of his own.

"You're broke," Nick said.

"I've got a new card coming," waving a hand. "Toys-R-Us rewards card. Should've been here today."

"I heard you talking to Felicia." He looked at Rizzo, then looked away. "How bad is it?"

Rizzo lifted an eyebrow, moved his mouth as if working through calculations. "A million is a round number." He tapped his cigarette with a finger and the ash fell gently into a bowl. He told Nick about the series of plots he had come up with throughout the past several months, plots he had recruited the other owners to join, guaranteeing quick returns on investments and repeating the phrase "no brainer" until he gave himself a headache. For instance: the sign spinner on the service road's curbstone. And the ensuing, and still ongoing, hospital bills. After a few shifts, the sign spinner had earned a brain-damaging heatstroke. Most recently Rizzo had found a Bulgarian marketing wizard online, convinced everyone in the business park to chip in for the not unreasonable fifteen grand upfront, and maybe it was a good thing they never heard from the marketing wizard after the first payment, Rizzo said—the wizard vanishing, that quick, with their money—because had he stuck around, they would've been duped into paying him another fifteen grand!

"I'll let Buford buy the business before the house goes to auction. It's simple," Rizzo said.

Silence. Then Nick, emotionless, head down, speaking to the table. "I keep asking myself why. Like, why am I still here? I died, I came back to life, but for what purpose? I'm a nobody. A loser. All the people who do not deserve to die—bring them back. But me?"

"I mean, when you put it like that."

A pair of headlights passed over the smoking men.

"I didn't even know I was dead." Nick pushed his hand through his hair, stared at the wall. "One second I'm in an apartment with my friends. Next I'm in a hospital bed. A nurse with a lazy eye is telling me I'm lucky to be alive, that my heart stopped for two seconds."

Rizzo, exhaling smoke: "There's no need to get emotional."

"After college I wanted to start a nonprofit, but there were so many logistics, rules. So I sat in front of a computer for ten hours too scared to move because I wanted my boss to know how hard I worked. And it never mattered. One of my bosses thought my name was Mikey." Nick stood, started to pace. "Rizzo's Firearms. Is it right for my dad to sell guns? Is it right for my dad to live in squalor? Is being homeless right?" Now, to Rizzo: "I'll help. I used to do this shit all of the time. SEO, SEM, CRM drips."

Rizzo hunched closer to the table.

"Okay?" Nick, less confident: "So, what do you think?"

"You've got a history of fuckups." Rizzo offered a palm to the air to conjure an example. "Remember the time I walked in on you with that girl? You two went to prom or homecoming or something together?"

Nick stopped pacing, scratched his beard. "I don't remember you telling me this."

"I came home early from the Chevy dealership." He nodded. "This was after I'd been selling those recyclable IV bags to the hospitals, but before I started selling those Shasta Jacuzzis to hotels. So the Chevy dealership. I came home early that day because I was getting my ass handed to me on the sales floor. Not interested after not interested." Rizzo, upset: "Even some ninety-five-year-old lady gave it to me up the ass that day. So I sped home and wanted to bang around in the garage to blow off some steam. Roundhouse the punching bag. Fill some shells on the bullet press." Voice higher: "Well, I open the garage and what do I see? I see your car there, Nick. Your car, in my spot. So I'm ready to lose it, and I go to your room, and I open the door, and I see you and this tan blond bombshell just going at it. I mean, first she's on top of you and it's like she's trying to fit your whole body inside her, like that's how bad she wants it. And then you're just really giving it to her from behind. And then she's sucking you off like she actually enjoys it."

"How long did you walk in on us for?"

Rizzo, to the ceiling: "I never landed a girl as good-looking as I saw in your room that day. So I think, Maybe that's why I suffered, my father suffered, my grandfather suffered, Uncle Gio, all the Rizzos. Maybe this is our legacy. All for me to witness my son get a blow job from a knockdown ten in Arizona. I think, Not so bad. I think, Probably worth it."

"Stacey. She rode horses in rodeos as a kid. Barrel-racing, they called it."

"And somehow you managed to fuck that up!" Here Rizzo's hands moved in circles as a sign of *how could you*.

Nick, deadpan: "For our entire senior year of high school she'd been cheating on me with Paul Bas. You remember Paul? My best friend from, what, sixth grade? His cock was about twice the size of mine. We used to joke about it in the locker room. Not only how big his cock was, but specifically how much bigger it was than mine. This while he was fucking my girlfriend."

"I remember his mom, Mrs. Bas. That's what I remember." He leaned forward in his seat. "There's a knockdown ten for you. A lawyer too no less. She gave my hand a real squeeze the one time I got myself in front of her in the stadium on one of those Friday nights. I'm so sorry, she kept saying. I had no idea what she was apologizing for. Maybe she thought I was David Goldstein, the guy whose autistic son got accidentally gobbled up by that tractor."

"How does this relate to the business?"

Rizzo stared at his son as if trying to remember. Then: "It establishes a pattern of behavior."

Nick, with a hand to his chest: "How about this: I'll take out a loan in my name. I'll take on all of the risk, Dad." He leaned forward, eyes wide, waiting. "Okay?" His voice was strained but steady: "Trust me."

Rizzo shook his head, stared down at his hands. Trust? He lit another cigarette. Trust his son? That was all he wanted, and he knew that to do so meant he was doomed.

8

Rizzo had learned from a voluble and mostly reliable source that the world's first case of agita occurred in his own family in 1944. The same source claimed that the entire philosophy of French existentialism had been developed not by German thinkers but, instead, by Italian Americans. Jean-Paul Sartre— "J.P. was what we called him"—stole the concept of agita, it was said, and renamed it nausea. Uncle Giovanni was the source.

Uncle Gio, an eccentric but genuine man, a true family pillar. He had lived on the first floor of a twelve-unit brick building with the brooding simplicity common to insane asylums. This was in Providence, Rhode Island, not far from Federal Hill, a neighborhood where red-sauce palaces lined the avenue. And here was Uncle Gio, an ambitious if misguided artist with a fascination for the city—or at least with a certain subset of the city's commuters. He took photos of women on public buses.

"Buses. Only buses," Uncle Gio said, swinging a hand through the icy air while with the other he cranked the steering wheel to parallel-park his epic Buick. "Women, buses. It's about the combination. It's about lust and reason. It's about the beauty of a stranger inside everyday technology. Technology so common, by the way, that we don't even think about a bus *as technology*. The ventilation, the windows, the seats, the air-pressured door. Don't get me started on the door!"

Adrift Uncle Gio, whose visits came without a call. He was the provider of bald truth, raw life. He paused on sidewalks to tell stories to strangers. He entertained those waiting in Sunday-breakfast lines. To him all was beautiful, all was worthy of remark. He wore a beret, leather jacket, wool slacks in the spring. He had a square meaty face with a swollen nose, his scalp proud beneath the few strands of combed black hair. He bragged about eating the same breakfast for three decades—two fried eggs, two sausages, two pieces of precisely buttered white toast—as he turned his eggs to coal with shaken pepper. Short but dense between the shoulders, he walked with the speed of someone far taller. He preserved a dignity in his solitude, in the slivered nights, talking of his past with such love that his loneliness seemed to be a choice.

Uncle Gio discovered agita during the Battle of the Bulge. He was there, he had told Rizzo, as another useless soldier to be shelled in the snow. Almost as soon as the shooting began he lost his battalion. How? If he knew he would have been able to find them! After firing a few shots through some trees, after leaning against an abandoned tank, he ran toward a group he thought were his allies, but then—realizing the group was instead a cluster of Nazis—he tried to run back the way he came, only to trip down a high snowbank, rolling over discarded weapons, broken branches, and corpses. He found himself on his back, in the muddy snow, exhausted, staring at his boots. His gun? Gone. Next to him was a group of French soldiers huddled over one of their dying own. Everywhere was exploding earth. He had fallen into a fight without a weapon. His allies were strangers he did not understand. Gunshots, shouted German. The naked woods, the solemn blue. Aircraft. All Uncle Gio could do was stare at his boots. How could this be his life? And what had it all been for? He was overcome with rage and anguish. There was supposed to be a dark nobility in death, but its prospect now brought only a deep burn to his chest. He was nothing, he realized. He was identical to all of these soldiers, one of a common category, and his purpose in life, if he survived this day, would be to go forth in search of a way to separate himself, to make himself more worthy of remembrance than his boots.

In this moment he named the feeling. Agita. It was not an intentional derivative of the Italian *agitare,* as many would later say. Rather, it was simply the sound that he was forced to release in response to the pain. Less word, more gasp. Agita. That it corresponded to *agitare* was a sign that his experience was more than coincidence—and it did not take long to realize that agita applied to crises far off the battlefield. For example: indigestion. When else do you feel more human—as in more aware of your mortal body, as in the material conditions of your existence, as in the absurd power of your insides—then after a massive meal?

All of this Uncle Gio told to his audience at Monsieur Billi, a red-lit bar on Rue Bonaparte, in the spring of 1945. The cosmopolitan group of about a dozen soldiers and grifters and broads included J.P., who was then known to Uncle Gio not as an ally who had survived capture by the Germans, nor even as an intellectual, but instead as a foolish snob in constant alarm over the actions of his creative love obsession, Simone de Beauvoir, whom Uncle Gio claimed to have known intimately on more than one occasion. ("We all did. That broad? Absolutely wild.") Notice the timing. The philosophic dialogues, led by Uncle Gio, took place throughout that spring at Monsieur Billi, less than a year before J.P. would deliver the lecture "Existentialism Is a Humanism," advancing his supposedly original idea that existence comes before essence—an idea that made J.P. a hero across America. Did it need to be spelled out? Uncle Gio had been ripped off by some French dandy with a silver spoon up his ass!

(Never mind that *Nausea* had originally been published in 1938. Never mind that *Being and Nothingness* had been published in 1943. Never mind, as a fellow Providence photographer, Dianne DeStrambano, had tried to tell Uncle Gio on more than one occasion, that Sartre had in fact ripped off Hegel and Husserl and Heidegger. Uncle Gio was certain. Agita explained all. And Sartre was, at a minimum, using agita to bolster that prim notion of nausea. So Uncle Gio would forever be overlooked for his contributions to Western philosophy. Which was a legitimate cause of agita.)

To avoid another situation like the one following his tumble at the Battle of the Bulge, in the dusk of his life Uncle Gio traveled everywhere with a gun. A revolver was packed along with his camera: a classic Ruger, stainless steel, a round chamber built to hold six gold bullets. Rizzo would never forget his introduction. In that Buick, in the northeast winter, their breath in clouds in the car while they sat parked, watching the buses come and go beside the glorious stone courthouse at Kennedy Plaza. Engaged in a monologue on technology, Uncle Gio reached across Rizzo, dropped open the glove box, retrieved the gun from where it was wrapped in a towel. It was a beauty that a young Rizzo would be unable to articulate to himself for some time, the beauty of sharing something more than a name with a person he loved. A family was not an accident—it was formed through shared pursuits, stories, objects, and here was theirs, Rizzo now understood, the Ruger. He was closer to his uncle Gio after that day, and his uncle Gio must have felt that way too, because he was clear about the future of the gun, one of the few possessions named in his will. The Ruger went to Rizzo.

It was a history that Rizzo now recalled with an intense and depressing gratitude. He was in bed, on his back, in much the same position he imagined Uncle Gio after his fall, and with agita to spare. It was as if his lungs were twisted around his heart. He blamed his son. He blamed Buford. He blamed himself. His room was dark and soundless. He listened for some noise from Nick, heard none. He grabbed his pack of Reds from the side table, sat up smoking in the shadows.

The business had been his chance to be more than another guy whose life came up soul-crushingly short. It was all Rizzo wanted. For his son, too. Together, they were to brandish a dynamic family crest.

But if he sold? No more worries about the house. Free. Except he'd need to appear at all the compounds of car dealerships again, bereft, a man near sixty with a slump and a slick back, cheery, humiliated, his name on a piece of paper above the word *experience*.

How stupid he had felt, those first years as a salesman: standing in front of some imposing home, balancing an unwieldy machine, waiting long after the doorbell chime. He had sold blenders, toasters, wood-fire pizza ovens, never-dulling knives, dishwashers and washing machines and microwaves and refrigerators; he had sold every type of car, minus the luxurious; worked nights, weekends, birthdays, Thanksgivings, overtime on Christmas Eve, up until the ball dropped for New Year's; more times than he could count he had been let go, terminated, relieved, dismissed, accused, accosted, and told to go fuck himself. He was willing to work, he was above nothing. But by the standards of bloated men he had been informed he was not good enough. He did everything he could to resist their conclusions.

It was more than five years since Uncle Gio passed. The call came from Cousin Jimmy. Guess what? The philosopher kicked the bucket. December funeral. Rizzo would have been to Providence in time for the ceremony, but the cheapest flight to T. F. Green had three connections—two of which, after a delay in Orlando, he missed. He got to town a day after his uncle had been buried. All the one-way streets were wet and the plowed snow formed barricades along the sidewalks. Above the sprawling homes converted into apartments the sky was a worn nickel. It had been so cold Rizzo felt a chill inside his ears.

"It's not like he knows you missed the funeral," Cousin Jimmy had said.

They were on Atwells at the Old Canteen. It had been Uncle Gio's favorite restaurant. (His decades-old order: polenta, veal and peas, a baked potato, then black decaf coffee.) The waiters all wore black suits and bow ties and were over the age of sixty-five. Each was assigned a teenaged busboy, all of whom wore white button-downs beneath expressions that were reliably terrified. It was Uncle Gio who had pointed out how the pairing had a religious quality, Rizzo had remembered. Not long afterward he began to weep. Rizzo, hunched, crying on the pink chair. All the leather cushions on the booths were pink—somehow, the entire restaurant was: the walls pink, two shades, same with the patterned curtains, lampshades, the napkins, the linen beneath the white tablecloths.

"Hey, pal." Cousin Jimmy was in a purple turtleneck and had his mustache trimmed above his lip. He was a former special ed teacher who now worked as a prison guard. He had given a crying Rizzo an elbow to the ribs, a comforting nod. He had flagged the waiter, ordered another round. Then, after Rizzo blew his nose in his napkin, Cousin Jimmy had asked: "Hey, just to confirm, dinner's on you, right?"

What Cousin Jimmy did not know was that Rizzo had been left by Allegra earlier that week. His Long Legs. His love. Gone. Left him not just for anyone, either, but for John Rubenstein, his boss at Mesa Mitsubishi. She took nothing. This hurt Rizzo the worst. There was no fight over the house, there was no fight over the furniture—she wanted nothing except to leave. John had been hired as the general manager of a Hyundai dealership in Prescott.

John and Allegra, up north together with nothing of Rizzo's, pleasant and apologetic and sadistic.

To Allegra, Rizzo understood, he had nothing worth taking, and that was how he knew she no longer loved him. Before the year had ended Rizzo remortgaged the house to buy his place in the business park property from Buford.

He got it, he did. Love was like money. It had to be earned.

9

It was not uncommon for Buford Bellum to be spotted in a corner booth at the Waffle House on McDowell and Eighty-third Avenue. There was an emotional significance to the space for Buford, which many found he was forthcoming about: it was here, at this exact Waffle House, where his career as an entrepreneur began. His first job at thirteen—leaning through the steam to scrape batter crust off the grill after he finished the dishes but before the trash. This exact location. From dishwasher to waiter, from waiter to manager, and then, after negotiating a favorable buyout plan: franchisee.

It was more than the teenage Buford Bellum had ever hoped for himself. In high school he suffered from the Trinity of the Virgin—he was fat, he had acne, and instead of a car he had a bicycle his perpetually shit-faced father had stolen from Sandra Day O'Connor High School's principal; a bicycle Buford continued to use, by the way, even after graduation, because the principal, Mrs. Sanchez, was too embarrassed to make him give it back, and Buford felt too ashamed to refuse her request that he keep the thing. So there went the humiliated teenager, in his apron and collared uniform, wobbling on a two-speed along the edge of the desert road.

But at the Waffle House all was different. At the Waffle House Buford was needed, acknowledged. They gave him overnights on Fridays and breakfasts on Sundays, he volunteered to switch to locations in Tempe. All of those who worked with the teenage Buford recalled his unusual diligence. Some said they felt pity for his pride in work that could not be more mindless, while others envied his unfaltering sense of purpose.

Whatever it takes for the dollar—it was a phrase his father, the tank-top orator, was known to repeat. So Buford took on any bet. Never mind the risk, never mind the purse. It was a daily occurrence at school. Hey, Buford, a dollar says you won't chug three cartons of maple syrup. Hey, Buford, two bucks you won't snort this line of salt. Hey, Buford, five bucks you won't sing the national anthem with that dead pigeon in your mouth. But he did and he did and he did. He was buttressed by the disgust he made for others. Believe whatever you want—he thought but did not say—because the future will be far kinder to Buford Bellum. Time would restore all sense of justice, of cosmic order. Or, if not, he would be so rich that it no longer mattered.

It was once Buford owned his first Waffle House location that he started flipping cars. He did it himself in the Waffle House parking lot. Buford outside in his visor and apron telling an old man in a safari hat that the lowest he could go on the Datsun was two grand. It became a weekend event that Buford advertised in *Auto Trader*: the end of the strip mall was now an unsanctioned car dealership packed every Sunday morning with minivans and trucks and rundown convertible coupes that Buford bought at auctions and now priced over twice what he paid but still half of what similar vehicles might cost anywhere else. He was a volume man. He worked harder and smarter. He sold a peeling two-toned Lincoln with bottles of the previous owner's ACE inhibitors in the glove box. He flipped a compact Ford truck with a fine leather cabin that had been the site of a double homicide. His best sale was the van designed to be wheelchair accessible. The van had an automatic door, a platform that lowered, in other words: necessary features for which he overcharged. He was not romantic. He was driven. Without fray or fluff in his speech, he promised to make people happy in a hurry. How about some waffles on your way out? And there they went, people wandering among the glaring cars, contemplating the interiors through the windshields, while Buford hustled from prospect to prospect, stopping to deliver orders via walkie-talkie to the Waffle House's on-shift manager when necessary.

The success from dealing cars was enough to buy up other Waffle House locations, which eventually allowed him to take over a dealership for used cars, motorcycles, and jet skis—along with several car washes— which financed his shift into land development. (It did not take long for the kid who had grown up in a desert unnoticed by the rest of the country to identify the subtle ingress of ambitious transplants under the age of fifty.) He bought a kingdom of crabgrass land: Apache Junction trailer parks, an assortment of homes at auction, shadowless acres ninety miles west of Phoenix; then he moved into insurance, construction, opened a construction equipment dealership, founded his own real-estate agency, a real-estate training program, a training program for real-estate agents on selling insurance between property closes; he bought a resort in Cabo San Lucas and founded a law firm that assisted exclusively in the cancellation of time-share contracts; he had an industrial cleaning service, a carpet installer, a tile company for floors and another for roofs, wind-shield repairs, an installer of pools and Jacuzzis, an exterminator chain that specialized in black widow spiders; there were countless strip malls, several daycares, a few golf courses, an after-school program embedded into the local school districts thanks to his well-documented donations, urgent-care facilities, two Methodist churches, plenty of All-American restaurants, a home health-care agency, multiple nursing homes—and Buford was said to have sold the first unit at his funeral-supply warehouse, South Phoenix Caskets, himself.

Here was the secret that drove the entire economy: the essence of everything was inefficiency. Each solution contained its very own problem, Buford knew, ensuring the market sustained itself by forever failing to satisfy its own promises.

Naturally Buford's ascent came with adversity. After a Bellum

investment became a disaster—leading to lawsuits, sell-offs, legal nego-
tiations with multiple grand juries—the used-car titan disappeared. Oh,
there were stories. Some said he was caring for his dying aunt. Others
insisted on an unfortunate turn during an aesthetic operation. There were
tabloid-style whispers about love children seeking hush money, unsigned
NDAs, rejected settlements, a new love interest with whom he was hiding
out in Santa Fe. A slightly less sensational take was that a stroke had
left him an enraged aphasiac. What all the stories had in common was
a crisis of the spirit that led to verifiable material losses: Buford Bellum
was briefly a victim of the same auctions that had made him rich.

All of which Rizzo learned from Felicia in patchwork fashion as he
sought a take two with the desert tycoon.

"The spares," Felicia said, out back, in the shade, in the regular
spot. She gave Rizzo a bag of browning lemons picked from her yard.
"Whatever takes your place, it'll be better than guns," she said. She wore
a hoodie and loose jeans. "I'd take a sex shop over guns," she said.

"That's my next endeavor," Rizzo said. "A sex toy emporium."

Which got him a croaky Felicia laugh.

Buford might be in his Waffle House of choice late tomorrow
night—or so Rizzo heard. Hence why he was in a denim shirt buttoned
to the top, scanning the diners. A man with an uneven buzz cut slouched
over a sad plate of toast, nodding off with his mouth open. A woman in
sunglasses and a snow jacket muttered to her reflection in the napkin
dispenser. The cook had his back to the room, flipping hash browns. And
there was Buford Bellum—holding a mug casually, the man was a figure.
Tall, broad, at ease, going soft with age but impressive all the same. His
hair was thick and gray and swooped. He wore a blue linen shirt with
the sleeves rolled up. He understood Rizzo's stare as a greeting. The boss
man raised his mug higher, gave a little nod.

"I've had plenty of help. Especially when things were tough," Buford
said, at the table. He spoke with a disarming humility, hands around his

coffee mug. It all made Rizzo want him to drop dead right here. "The worst investment of my life," Buford continued, "should've been the safest one."

A copper mine in Cananea, Mexico. The desert of Cananea was far different from Arizona, Buford said. Far less sharp. Miles of sand. Fading roads cut down toward the site of extraction. After the first and only rain of the summer a mist covered the land, the vapor rising from the rim of the mine like a searching cloud.

Burford said he bought the mine despite its history of disaster. There had been a short-lived workers' strike there in 1906: Mexicans lowered in cages through the sweltering dust of industry were paid half of what the white Americans were, so three thousand organized, and when their demands went predictably unmet, they gathered in the downtown of Cananea, near an American-owned wood shop, which they unpredictably lit on fire, burning four to death inside, inspiring Arizona Rangers to charge on horseback across the border. The effect was identical to the cause: Mexicans, paid less, lowered back into twisting sediment, toward the clamorous glint of rock-covered copper.

Less than a year into Buford's restoration, a child went missing in the mine. Which was a tragedy, yes, but one Buford thought he could overcome with a cash infusion. He had a helicopter lower him into the city, and he was taken by Jeep to the work site, where men played cards in front of single-wide trailers while news crews reported on the efforts of the search. A silence issued from the parked trucks and shovels. But even an offer from Buford to sign several blank checks—he had already invested thirty million dollars into the mine's expansion—was not enough to convince authorities to resume production. The missing child was the mayor's daughter. The Policia Federal opened no less than two dozen investigations. Active bribery, in various counts. This meant forced stoppages of Buford's operating investments all across northern Mexico. It did not take long for him to conclude that he was ruined.

"It was a source of great shame," Buford continued. "I'd never considered that I could fail." But then a former competitor in the world of venture capital reappeared, Stan Martin, a tiny Texan in pinstripes who was descended from old oil money and had turned his attentions to tech. "Stan wanted to bring me on as an expense consultant for some of his most high-risk investments. Figured I was positioned better than some McKinsey Ivy Leaguer who never worked before the age of twenty-two. He was right, but it was hardly flattering. To work for a man I'd competed against? A man whose vision I had no respect for? In an industry I thought was snake oil?" And yet that's exactly what Buford did, he told Rizzo. Humbled himself. Erased his ego. Leveraged the opportunity to build himself back.

"My point is that you're making a sound business decision. Even if it feels like a loss," Buford said. He indulged the moment with a long sip of coffee.

"I know that," Rizzo said.

"You got in over your head." Buford shrugged in a way that evidently meant Rizzo was not supposed to be offended by this. "I've seen it plenty of times. You had a midlife crisis, started to wonder about your legacy. But all things considered, you'll be making out okay. When I first sold you the place, it was far below fair market value. A good time to buy means a bad time to sell." An insight which led Buford to reflect aloud on recent real-estate transactions. There was the fifty acres out in Avondale to the Hyatt Regency. The Chandler fitness center bought by Crunch. The dental offices in the south valley that he unloaded on a California DSO for six times what he had paid. Oh, and the microchip manufacturer that went to Honeywell.

"You're doing all right," Rizzo said.

Buford had his phone out, scrolling. "Rizzo's Firearms. I'll need to change the name. Any recommendations?"

Outside, in the parking lot, Nick sat on a curb, lighting up a cigarette.

Before he could finish his drag, he got a slap on the back of his head from his father. "Let's go," Rizzo said, stepping between cars.

"So?" No answer. "What's the deal?" They were inside the Cadillac, buckling up.

"The deal," Rizzo said, turning the key in the ignition. He stared at his son. "I've made the executive decision that Buford Bellum will not be buying my shop."

Rizzo's expression was powerfully still. But as he turned the wheel, shifting quickly into drive, he bit his bottom lip and nodded to the silence.

10

If emotion defined life, then Rizzo could now consider himself excessively alive. Overwhelmed, he worried he was about to short-circuit.

The neurologist sat on a tiny stool, measuring Rizzo's pupils. His name was Dr. Kapoor and he had thoroughly white hair. Nick was in the room, squinting at a plastic model of a human brain missing a frontal lobe. There was a struggle: with his glasses on, Dr. Kapoor leaned toward one half of Rizzo's face, leaned back on his stool, then repeated the same movement with his glasses off. This continued for several rounds, unnerving Rizzo. Eventually Dr. Kapoor spoke. "What do you think?" That was his question.

Later that day Rizzo was in the shop shouting into his landline. The potential customer on the other end had questions only loosely related to the information Rizzo labored to deliver. "But what exactly does Ralph look like?" And then: "Lobster from where?" And: "Oh, so you mean the Pizza Hut." Rizzo launched into precise descriptions of impossible details. Look for the fire hydrant with the unhooked chain. That splayed quail corpse? The saguaro with only one bloomed bulb?

The caller had hung up.

Nick was behind the counter, sweeping the floor tiles. He was sweeping incorrectly. "Hey," Rizzo said, waving a hand. Nick gave him the broom and Rizzo showed him how. It was just a broom, just a routine task, draining and endless and never noteworthy—but he loved the sound of the brush gently touching the tiles. He had done this so often he no longer needed to think about its elements—the narrow stance, shoulders high, left hand forward and right hand back, all wrists—and instead could indulge the comfort he felt collecting the faint dust into a pile. The sound soothing, true. Rizzo turned to give the broom back to Nick but the kid was gone. Out front, smoking.

"I'm thinking," Nick said, when Rizzo leaned outside. His sandal tapped the ground, his hands were on his hips. There was a heavy shadow across the concrete from the far column of the strip mall. A curb surrounded a pile of orange pebbles, behind which stood a spry palo verde.

"Keep this in mind," Rizzo said. "The problem has been that there's no one in the shop for me to sell to. I'm a hell of a salesman." Wistful: "There was this afternoon in Seoul, in the Army, I was short for a drink, so I sold a blind homeless Korean guy prescription glasses for the money."

"Oh?"

Rizzo, now excited: "The way I sell is I stay amorphous. You wouldn't talk to a blind homeless Korean guy the same way you talk to a knockdown ten with legs up to here, right? Exactly. So my strategy is, amorphous. Fluid. I keep neutral, ask questions, figure out the person I'm talking to, what moves the needle. Plus, people think I'm stupid. Good. That's my big advantage. I let them think I'm stupid. I advance that narrative. I nod a lot. I take their shit, is what I'm saying. Then I come back with the routine. I raise my voice, gesture, do accents. I can be a cowboy and an Indian. I can be an aw shucks howdy do or a bing bang boom."

"The shop is hard to find," Nick said. "Also, there's like way more competition than I expected."

"Okay?" Rizzo, as if this was obvious. "Help people find it. Beat the competition." In silence he returned inside to reorganize the shotguns. An unfortunately timed decision, because it was while balancing an armful that his first chance for a sale in some time walked in. His name was Kurt Greenson. He was a bald man with a pitifully round face. His polo was tucked into his jeans, his boots were made for rigorous trails.

Kurt said he had been to about eight shops across the valley looking for this particular carbine, a rare achievement in ballistics craftsmanship, eight pounds of carbon fiber and titanium: the long-barrel G2, a hunting machine. Called earlier for directions. Poor connection. Ha, ha. Sure had a tough time finding the place.

"*Machine*," Rizzo said, repeating the word the guy had used instead of *gun*. Of course Rizzo had that machine. It hung on a wall with the other rifles.

The gun was black and lightweight and inconsistently angular.

Rizzo stayed silent as he handed over the G2, knowing this was not someone who needed to be sold. "Amazing," Kurt said, taking aim at the door, before he handed the gun back to Rizzo. "Just what I hoped for." Rizzo said he would ring it up, unless Kurt wanted to see a camo carrying case—but that wouldn't be necessary, Kurt said, since he was still doing research. Research? Yes, research. This was a step in the right direction, but now he wanted to read a few more reviews, return to the message boards.

Rizzo wanted to weep. Instead he spoke rapidly about features of the weapon: the aerograde carbon fiber, the stainless flash hider, the direct-impingement gas system, a match-grade trigger. "Match-grade," Rizzo repeated, louder. He now stood between Kurt and the exit. As he attempted to leave, Kurt commended Rizzo's knowledge. "My guess is that this thing will be gone by the end of the day," Rizzo said, as Kurt shuffled past. Then, a last shot: "I can come down on price!" But Kurt was gone. And who else should be holding the door open for him? Nick, in the entryway. Rizzo stared down to his own hideous fingers. The only thing worse than speaking was saying nothing at all. No one had told Rizzo how lonely it was to grow old.

"I'll need, like, a week," Nick said, on his way by. "Before I show you what I've got, I mean."

The soonest a new neurologist could see Rizzo, however, was four months from now, by which point he would be dead. So Rizzo settled for a cardiologist. In the waiting room he listened to a man on the phone describe the increased cost for first-class flights. "What I would do to see someone with an actual condition," the cardiologist said, while jabbing electrodes on Rizzo's chest. Rizzo was on his back, on the bench, shirt open, embarrassed and wincing. "Heartburn. Anxiety. That's all I see now." She was a tall dark woman with rimless glasses. "If I'd known when I was in medical school," she said, "I would've become a psychologist!" The doctor told Rizzo about her brother-in-law, who was only an LCSW—but charged three hundred bucks a session and could afford to spend six weeks in Mykonos—as she reviewed the results. "This says you had a heart attack," waving a piece of paper, "but it's wrong ninety-nine percent of the time," before sending him to another room for a precautionary echocardiogram.

While the technician talked about the beauty of Arizona compared to his native New York, he showed Rizzo his heart. "Every day is majestic," the technician said. And then, nodding toward the screen: "We use Doppler." Rizzo, on his back again, with a harsh turn of his neck to see: a vague triangle rippled. "Everyone has something," the technician said, "but you're fine." What Rizzo heard was that he would most certainly die.

That evening Bill Friar, again dressed as a monk, performed a range of nebulous karate moves in aisles lined with unhung pendant lamps. He was defeating all of the dark energy. The ad closed with Bill in a white suit, standing on a cloud, a direct address. If you need ceiling fans or chandeliers or sconces. If you are in search of pharmacy floor lamps. Bill Friar has swing arms, modern arcs. He has torchieres. Twenty-five percent off anything in the store with the purchase of a Rockin' Monks T-shirt. New location in Ahwatukee. Remember—and here a shadowed landscape appeared on the screen before a burst of neon—go toward the light!

Rizzo held a plate for burgers and another for corn, had a cigarette behind an ear and a grill lighter pinched under an elbow. If he had a free hand, he would have used it to throw the remote at the television.

The colonoscopy and the endoscopy both came back clean, and yet the gastroenterologist recommended they test motility through an anorectal manometry. The third primary-care doctor was congratulatory about the status of Rizzo's prostate but wanted him to consider cryolipolysis—to remove some average but unsightly belly fat—for two thousand dollars a treatment. The bone spurs he had never before noticed could be managed with orthotics, the podiatrist said, and those cost a mere six hundred bucks. The dentist recommended more floss, and laser whitening. The naturopath in Glendale sold him half a grand worth of vitamins. All the additional opinions more or less matched the originals. He had soon been to a dozen doctors with his son in tow and still not met his deductible.

"You surround yourself with guns and then wonder why you're nervous," Felicia said. She pointed at Rizzo with her cigarette hand. "I gave you a way out, remember?" They were behind the shop, on their lawn chairs, smoking in the morning sun. Felicia took out her phone, jabbed at the screen with a finger. "Meditation doesn't make you less rude, Rizzo. Ronny can't help you with that."

A portion of freeway separated two versions of the desert: to the west were billboards for immigration lawyers, divorce lawyers, injury and accident lawyers, DUI lawyers, a spine institute with lasers that were minimally invasive; warehouses, graffitied lots, flat brick buildings, a carpet installer beside a steelworks, drainage canals that had known nothing but dust; the shallow brown water of a town lake, then construction sites more common than the palm trees—the excavators surrounded by orange fencing, the piles of earth, rotating cement mixers at the edges, and everywhere the promising skeletons of houses and apartments and condos—while to the east, nothing but artichoke land: the striations of the buried vegetables continued into blue oblivion.

Ronny Deloitte lived several miles outside Globe. The town had a main street of dead shops before a thriving buffet. Rizzo and Nick shook in the Cadillac down the dirt road that led to the trailer, which was parked in the shadow of a crimson mesa. White sheets—hung on a clothing line strewn between cacti—offered an eerie flatness, and the steel beams of the silent wind chimes were mirrors for the sunlight. "I'm done trying to heal. You can tell Felicia that too," Ronny said. He stood on the porch in a kimono. "What has healing others ever done for me? I got into law school yesterday. I'm thinking tax. That's where the money is."

A stalwart woman in the checkout line spoke about the rising price of bananas. The man in a bad suit at the next gas pump over argued about the cost for the hotel in West Palm. In the AutoZone waiting area, crying out his request for a dollar, a child pointed at the vending machine. The prices leaped out in the aisles, on the roadways, from the voices on the radio, every screen. There were numbers, there was nothing else. Money lost, money saved. Even his son. He took out some loans. Welcome to the club! But Rizzo had to hear about it during dinner at Hector's BBQ—hear about it while, also, listening to a family, at the next table, enumerating on the bill each item and its cost.

Nick was dedicated to the business. He was also erratic, and not particularly effective. But he was committed. And from all signs sober. None of the past evidence of a slip: no idiot friends, in hats and sunglasses, waiting at the door; no unjustifiably long stays in the bathroom, filling the tub but coming out dry; no straw-and-tinfoil ball in the laundry. And yet Rizzo felt an unabating suspicion toward the actions of his son, as if each gesture, each movement, each word or errand would be the last, the one Rizzo would need to recall when his son was soon gone.

Nick on the computer. Nick pacing the hall. Nick in a doorway, flustered. Nick, on the patio, sitting with his legs crossed, wasting away in the grueling afternoon. Knocking on the top hinge of a door with the tip of a screwdriver. In the garage, hands on his hips, staring at a steel dumbbell between his bare feet. Midday on a yoga mat, on the living room floor, watching the ceiling fan wobble to a stop. Kneeling before the router and modem, unplugging wires, waiting. Late at night, Rizzo up for a piss and a drink, and there was his son in the kitchen in the dark, the refrigerator light on his helmet of hair. Up, still, why? Can't sleep, don't know, never a why. Doing what? Nothing. Nothing? Turning from the fridge, his son, in the frightening appliance light.

Nick shirtless, shadowed, running water. He seemed stunned by the sink, the faucet's dribble against the basin. In his hand, a red plum. Sad fruit, with a stubborn knotted stone, turning beneath the water.

His child as a burned man on a median holding out a sign for spare change—this was what Rizzo feared. But so long as he could see his child now all might be okay. So he brought an intensity, a sense of study, to each look he gave his son. He did not think of the kid as an extension of himself, a way to live on. Nico was a man of his own. Regardless of whether Rizzo lived. And that seemed more unbelievable. A person, existing, because of Rizzo. A person, surviving, in spite of Rizzo. Life was impossible—this fact made all things incredible.

Or so Rizzo concluded while in the shop cleaning today. He dragged an old milk crate over, sat next to a case of handguns, sprayed the surface and wiped it dry with a rag. He liked the squeak, he liked the fading print on the glass.

The bell above the door rang: a stringy guy, walking toward the counter with an awkward wave.

His name was Steven. He was pale, reddish. He wore a loose button-down and was looking for a fifty-caliber assault-style rifle. The, like, Beowulf?

The gun hung on a wall cluttered with other tactical rifles. The dinosaur hunter, Rizzo called it. Was it possible that a stranger found his way to the shop to purchase a three-thousand-dollar rifle at first sight?

Rizzo wanted to call Nick in from the warehouse to see, but he stayed silent as he took down the embarrassingly cumbersome weapon. Tried to tug back the charging handle—tried, and struggled. Rizzo offered a laugh and rested the stock of the gun on his stomach, then used all of his strength to pull the handle.

Chamber cleared.

Rizzo situated Steven for a proper hold. They stood together on the carpet, one behind the other, as he nudged Steven's boots farther apart, then flicked the kid's back elbow. Silence. Rizzo wanted the weight of the gun to be known. The view down the iron sights, the notch near the top of the barrel for aim. He did not list the many details worth celebrating: the two-part receiver modularity, threaded muzzle, stock spring to absorb the shock, the power to fire hundreds of rounds in minutes. Instead Rizzo whispered one question: "How does it feel?"

The card was charged and the door was closed and Rizzo, alone, gave the air a series of fist pumps.

But the sense of celebration ended when, wanting to be sure his son overheard, Rizzo popped into the warehouse and found no Nick. Rizzo called out in an attempt to retrieve his child from the abyss. Nick!

"One sec" was what he heard. In the far corner of the warehouse a block of light filled the doorway.

A waiting Rizzo stared between the tall steel shelves. There was a cot with a pillow but no blanket for when he was too tired to make the drive home. The electric razor that often left him with the same scruff but also a chin of dried blood. A rubber ball that made all body-weight exercises more intense—push-ups, sit-ups—which, beside his desk, was layered in dust. Underneath the cot, a wood case of collectible silver coins he had been bulled into buying by an infomercial numismatist. As Rizzo listened to Nick's sandals slide closer, the objects of his office had never felt farther away.

All was meaningless without his son.

11

Open on the desert. Purple monsoon clouds, shrubby creosote. Nothing else on the horizon but a spindly cactus withered brown. Anticipation radiates from the compact miles. Lightning, long rumble. The crash of rain now forms gray sails in the sky. Another bolt cracks across the mountains. We zoom.

"Zoom?" Rizzo interrupted.

Zoom, Nick repeated. A building emerges. It's the business park. Still shot of Rizzo's Firearms. Suddenly the rain stops, replaced by delirious desert sunshine. Inside the shop, there's a panoramic view of the inventory. A muscular man is behind the counter. Across his barrel chest he holds a lever-action rifle, the gun that gives shape to the Wild West. In a button-down and checkered slacks he looks like a mix of the Rock and Sylvester Stallone, but less dumb. This is the actor playing Rizzo.

"Why can't I be me?" Rizzo asked.

Next to Rizzo is Nick, who, playing himself, is clean-shaven and does not look remotely like a bum. Cue the spotlight. Staring straight into the camera, Nick delivers a monologue. He believes in the monologue. Reality is made by testimonials. He tells the camera about the sobriety brought on by joining his father's business. His new gun hobby saved his life, offered him purpose, community, responsibility. The gun is a talisman. The gun saved him not only from the world, but from himself. The gun equals life. And the best way to defend this life, Nick concludes, is with a gun from Rizzo's Firearms.

"Also, TV is way cheaper than the digital stuff I've been working on," Nick said.

"I like the idea," Rizzo said. "My problem is the visuals."

They were at the table, father and son, both smoking. It was the hour of pink skies—almost gone for the day, the sun cast its final colors, which spread through Rizzo's yard to the vertical branches of the ocotillo. A neighbor removed ironwood leaves from his driveway, cautiously shifting the blower through the air. Rosebushes trembled in the warm winter light.

Nick twisted his cigarette in an ashtray, lit another. "We want the infomercial feel. The visual cues need to be cheap, minimal. We want humble and holy and accessible. To buy a gun is to acknowledge the possibility of your own death. To acknowledge, but to then deny that possibility. To buy a gun is to insist on life. A major decision, but not one only for those who can pay major prices. We want the ad to look cheap—cheap, but righteous. Cheap because righteous? The right gun, the right choice, the right cause. We should play into that more. Fear. That's most important. The more people own guns, the more gun ownership makes sense."

Rizzo leaned back in his chair, arms crossed. How could his son not see? "The afterlife angle," Rizzo said. "Let's give you angel wings, a halo. Let's get you talking about the resurrection."

"There is no afterlife angle."

"Of course there is," shrugging. "What do you mean? You died, Nick. You must've seen something while you were dead. Let's get that in here. Let's make good use of the greatest mystery to mankind."

Nick, eyes closed, annoyed: "I understand having questions, Dad, but I don't have anything insightful for you."

"It's not for my sake—other people, they want to know."

"Who?"

"Who doesn't, Nick? I mean, that would be a shorter list. One sentence, I saw blank—you're a millionaire. You write a book. Autobiography.

What I saw while I was dead. Fucking millions is how much people would pay to hear."

"Except as I've said, I didn't see anything, so I have nothing to say. That would be my autobiography. *Nothing to See Here.* That's a good reason to appreciate life, a good enough reason for me, at least, to want to stay sober, make work meaningful, because I know there is nothing else."

"Memories," Rizzo said. "I hope it's memories. Like the day when I got back from the service. My mother tied ninety-nine balloons all around the porch. My father called the *Cranston Herald*. A reporter was there in the yard to take a photo. I was in my Green Beret uniform because I wanted to show off. My dog Major, he was a border collie, oh, he was the best, and he was out in the yard too."

Rizzo had been most excited to see Major. He couldn't help it. He kept a photo of his dog in his pocket. He stepped out of his father's car and just tackled the dog right there, they were rolling, biting, laughing in the yard. Rizzo's beret fell off. He had never been happier to return to that haunted place called home. But all the sudden he felt whacks against his ribs. What in the goddamn hell? *Whack whack whack.* Well, the whacks were from his father, who got the rake and started hitting Rizzo and telling him to stand up because he was embarrassed about how excited Rizzo was to see the dog instead of his mother. His father wanted him to run out of the car to hug his mother. Again, his father said. The arrival the reunion everything. The reporter said hey that's okay this is good, but his father said good I'll give you good go stand over there numb-nuts and wait for my cue. And his mother said Jesus Christ, come on. And his father said don't Jesus Christ me or you'll get the rake next. So his mother and the reporter stood there terrified while his father made Rizzo get back in the car and they drove around the block and his father told Rizzo how to exit the car and approach his mother for the photo and how to arrange his face so it looked especially happy and so on and so forth.

"And that's what I want to remember," Rizzo said. "Not the last part. Not the rake part. Not me and my father in the car practicing happy faces at each other. I want to remember me, back from the service, in my uniform, on the lawn, with my beautiful dog Major."

"But dad, that's what I saw."

"Excuse me?"

"A dog. A border collie. Black and caramel. A dog sitting with his tongue out beneath a spruce tree. He said, 'My name is Major.'"

"Hey, Nick," with a smile. "That's hilarious."

"'My name is Major,'" Nick said. "'I was your father's dog. You are no longer living. I have come to you with a message.' And then he led me through the afterlife and I experienced true self-discovery and changed for the better."

"Well, it's been decided," Rizzo said. He had his hands behind his head. "Back from the dead, but fortunately still an asshole. This is how I know God is real: my son who makes me laugh."

12

Memories? Why memories? It was the television, Rizzo knew. From the screen he learned to expect a final reel before the end.

He wanted Nick as a kid at the apartment complex with the pool. The Princess, they called it. Smashed together half-homes of sand-pink concrete. The school bus stopped between speed bumps, picking up the kids. But the weekends, the bean-shaped blue. Three feet in the shallow end. The water overtreated with chlorine, the sting and stick. Doors slamming. Mariachi from one unit, and Zeppelin from another. Who could hold their breath the longest? This was the competition. Nick's idea, amazed at the idea of not needing air. Allegra on a rubber-stripped lounge chair, bikini afternoon, licking her thumb to crease the page of a *People*. Elbows on the stone rim. Nick beneath the water reaching, his limbs an unorganized swirl, slowing himself in laboring to be fast. Uneasy ovals of light off the water.

He wanted Rhode Island again. Scenes from an outdoor childhood. Woods and evolving clouds. Fireflies, mosquitoes, scrunching centipedes. Pollen itchy on the eyes. Running through a sudden rain that soaked through jeans to the skin. The wind-bent reeds that lined the curved road to the beach. White waves, white sand. Sunburns and fireworks. Blasting his feet with cold water from the spigot. Around dreary Ralph's Diner, the fog of an August morning. Saint Matthew's with the deadly sharp steeple. Main Street, its only red light dangling in the hard wind before a storm. Heart-attack Greg, a cigar locked in his lips, raking the orange leaves in the dim hours. Bambalean, Rizzo's mother said. The welcome chaos of Sunday dinner. Papa Bob, parked on a chair in front of the oven door, a rag over his shoulder, and the sharp parting of the cousins in the hall when he waddled past holding high the steaming green glass tray of veal meatballs. Plates of soft wedding cookies, biscotti, zeppoles, pizzelles. Powdered sugar stuck to bunched Saran wrap. Shadows of the winter trees trafficking across the silent road at sunset. The year the snow reached to the doorknobs. Iced-over lake, ice-struck windows, hellish hail across the packed clapboard. A world no cars moved through, the smack of the shovels at dusk. In the driveway, their Plymouth, the exhaust and headlights.

He wanted his father, Rocco. He was a man solicited for his sideways takes. Same with his mother. What she said. Anne Marie the shoe seller. Bring her back. Gossiped as she hauled her bulk before a customer, kneeling to shove a high heel on over the swollen pantyhose of a stranger. They talked and talked, his parents, but little Rizzo spilled hardly a word. He wanted to be the kid wandering the woods in freedom again, the wind dragging sticks through the leaves. He wanted those days, those days alone and free.

When Rizzo flew off at eighteen—how could he forget? Special Forces. Green Beret. To parachute out of a plane through the choking darkness. Fort Bragg. To fall from a plane, spin through the air, alone except for a bag attached to your back. He was young and too stupid to be afraid. All the parachuting soldiers were like plummeting bits of cloud. Rizzo, crouched in the armpit of the jungle, with a hangover, waiting for two months for a boat that never came. Nicaragua, sunrise. He could go without that. The cigar factory, a mass of concrete that held a greenish light above the brackish water. Tangled mangroves. Leafy banana trees. Salt mist off the tide. Honorable discharge. His fatigues he folded neatly in a box he intended to never open. Home, again. All sense of purpose drained from the hideous woods. The salt-caverned sidewalk, the cold

May rain. In his unchanged childhood room he screamed through the night. His mother told him. No memory of the screams. He woke at strange times needing to sprint down the street but was restrained by the knowledge that he could not move his limbs, so he stayed flat in bed, in the lost morning, his heart slamming his sternum. In the grocery store people looked at him and said things as if he was actually there.

He wanted back his job sweeping the factory floor of swarf, alone at night directing his broom across the even epoxy, the too-small shards that glittered. He wanted his Legs. His love. Allegra Constantino. He wanted that brief but lucky overlap when he was finishing third shift and she was starting on first: the redhead with the smile on the sanding line, her protective glasses too big for her long face. Perfect on her backless stool, swiping fast, whistling while she worked. That lamp on the desk, and Rizzo, pushing the trash can by, paused to turn the bulb toward the ceiling. Yelling over the rip of tools. She got regular Coke from the vending machine, tore the tab from the can and dropped it in the soda as they walked next to the low brick wall that bordered the silent woods. Nothing, saying nothing, but smiling, laughing. Why? They fucked with random pieces of clothes on, looking at each other, while the window ACs beat all down the block.

Allegra's idea to move? No. The first days in Arizona? Maybe. How she weaved while she talked both hands through her heavy hair? Yes. How she became a kindergarten teacher, and she loved their son, and she believed things could be fixed? Never mind.

How could there be no afterlife?

Rizzo was in bed, sleepless, ragged, staring at the ceiling in the dark. He suddenly felt as if he neared the finish of all things.

It was not that Rizzo had been so sure about what followed his time—though he could not help but hold out hope for heaven—but his prior uncertainty of what came after death at least helped with the fear. Hope rose when he did not know. But his son knew, his son had died, and he insisted that what followed in no way resembled the cloud palace that Rizzo as a kid in church had thought of as the afterlife.

But how could this be it? How could this be all he had? The simple biology that ruled his life was ridiculous, the lack of grace an incredible crime.

How could he be anything but terrified?

Outside, there was a cold sting to the air. Rizzo felt this in his lungs as he took another breath. He was not smoking. He would quit smoking. He was outside after midnight in his underwear and felt certain another cigarette was not in his future. Now, yes, the first without. He smelled the dust on the agave leaves. He looked up into the sky, at the patterns of stars, at the gold hooked moon.

13

There was a short truck in the next lane, its bed low from the unforgiving weight of men, about six guys with their heads down, their elbows on their knees, hunkered against the speed of the slicing wind.

The truck disappeared into the morning darkness at the next exit, but the Eldorado still rattled along at high speeds.

Rizzo rolled up his window, lit his first cigarette—he was down to half a pack a day. Nick pressed buttons on the dash to flip through radio channels. They drove early to the shop to feed the cats.

From the freeway a golf course gave way to shrubby terrain. Headlights. Long paths of shadow. Clouds unfurled above the mountain-wrapped land.

This was what Rizzo had long waited for: father and son, together, destined for somewhere. It was a reason for joy on the road. He was grateful for simple details. The cream swirled to sand in coffee. The weight in a room before sunrise. An instant ceremony from the powered-on television. Rituals, repeating, to orchestrate the days. Peaceful, these details were to Rizzo, because their appearance promised another continuation: the home, their family.

Like any true routine, the events of their mornings passed without discussion. There were fragments. Grunts. Curses of obstinate phone alarms. Rizzo fought to relax his limbs. He spun his arms, twisted at the waist, grimaced, bent his knees as he fought toward his toes. Slices of unbuttered wheat toast. He grabbed the black bread from the toaster and tossed a slice to his son. A meal on the move. They stepped around each other in the kitchen with a sleepy firmness. Each had a forty-ounce plastic cup, and Nick piled ice in each container, breathing loud as the water hit the cubes. Half-dressed, unashamed, Nick mumbling as he slid an arm through a shirt in front of the microwave. The garage smells of dust, rubber, exhaust. And the heartening clunk before the garage door rose to reveal the early asphalt. It was as if conversation would shatter the pleasant spell of beginning. They seemed to move in the wake of a wholly calming song.

Nick snatched the bag of cat food from the trunk of the Cadillac, spilling pellets across the parking lot. The sun was over the McDowell Mountains, the banded light pinkish high up but near white closer to the rock. The surprising green of the desert: spurts of deer grass, fountain grass, ruellia, yucca. The Arizona land known for its space, for what it was not, but still bristling with life. Rigid saguaros. Boulders were traced with purple Chihuahuan sage and fluffs of trailing rosemary. In the sand mounds home to rattlesnakes, black-throated wrens searched the earth for some beetle with which to zip off toward the thin streaks of cloud. The heat blended colors and forms as Nick walked to where the cats hid.

They cleaned each morning as if they had not picked up the broom in months. Rizzo liked the sight of his son polishing a surface. Nick, on a knee, stretching a rag across the glass panel above the handguns. They worked in silence: sweeping, dusting, reorganizing. Waiting. They broke down boxes, stepping on the creases of the cardboard.

And then, unprovoked, unfaltering, only on the morning drives, Nick began to talk about his life. The period for Rizzo that had been a blank now acquired detail, depth, proportion—all of which made it that much more frightening.

What happened to his child?

Nick, in an apartment off Baseline, when his sponsor overdosed, and someone proposed they call an ambulance, and someone else proposed they run, so Nick and his friends stumbled down the stairs and across the street to Tiki Rob's, the bar where they nodded off in the irregular light from the busted disco ball, waiting out the sirens. Nick and friends, sleeping in the office of a chiropractor off Northern. Nick, sneaking onto the tarmac—the roasted atmosphere across the Sky Harbor runways—to steal luggage from the trucks. An organ farm in a neglected plane hangar where surgeons operated on addicts. The strip-club owner who watched live surveillance footage of the dancers from his living room, blowing lines with whomever wandered in, while his wife sat parked in her wheelchair. There were hours in bathrooms at gas stations, In-N-Out Burgers, sushi restaurants. There were updates on kids Nick ran around with in high school. Brett Redson, the constant beneficiary of neighborhood charity, was strangled to death with a shoelace less than halfway through his eight-year sentence for aggravated robbery. Marcus Lintel, the college football star, now a car washer on the weekends, got so high that he passed out on top of his newborn daughter. Still, Nick missed some of his old friends. But he never called, never texted. He felt bad, guilty. He was scared. He thought to make himself new he needed to strip away his past. He was clean, he would stay clean.

He wanted his father to know that he was done fucking up.

14

(Beige wall cluttered with rifles: hunting rifles, assault
rifles, short-barrel rifles; rifles with bolts, scopes, laser
sights, extended clips; AR-15s, AK-47s, PTR-91Fs; rifles
from Heckler & Koch, BAE Systems, Marlin and Mannlicher,
CZ and Kel-Tec, Remington and Robinson and Sterling,
Tikka, Walther, Mossberg and Schweizerische Industrie-
Gesellschaft. Between guns, pinned high center, American
flag. In front of wall, glass case not unlike that of
jeweler, except in case is assortment of revolvers,
pistols, tactical knives with ribbed blade bottoms. In
front of glass case, NICK. Black polo, jeans, loafers.
His face pale from a fresh shave. His hair is slicked. He
scratches his neck, looks at camera, and then looks up at
ceiling. Outside frame, voices. NICK tries to cough, rubs
hands together. Unbuttons top of polo. Rubs hands across
stomach. Buttons top of polo. Stares, mouth open.)

                         NICK
     Hi I'm Nick Rizzo, of Rizzo's Firearms. Located just
     off Cave Creek and the 101, we're a family-owned
     firearm retailer with an affordable yet rare selection

of weapons and accessories. What separates us from all
the other gun dealers in the desert, though, is our
commitment to combatting opioid addiction. Here in the
desert we've all felt the effects of addiction on our
friends, coworkers, and families, and we at Rizzo's
Firearms intend to do our part. So every time you buy
one of our Colts, LaRues, Beowulfs, Brownings, H and
Ks, Ithacas—even if you just stop in to pick up one of
our custom-colored laser sights, a box of birdshot,
buckshot, wad cutters, slugs—every time, we'll donate
a percentage of the sale to a local rehab center.
See, opioid addiction is an issue that hits home
for us at Rizzo's Firearms. I'm a recovering heroin
addict. Not long ago, in fact, I overdosed and died.
You heard that right: died. And it was then that my
father, David Rizzo, decided to, planned to—

    (stares at ceiling)

Opioid addiction is an issue that hits home for us at
Rizzo's Firearms. I'm a recovering that died with an
addict—

    (stares at ceiling again)

A recovering dead—

    (stares at ceiling while muttering)

I'm a recovering addict. And not long ago I, well. I
died. I overdosed, and then died, and now here I am.

*(Beyond the lights, the key grip, the camera operator, the
director, a crowd fills the aisles in unassessed silence.
They watch from the shadows. FELICIA, stepping between
shelves of bullet boxes, stepping between people, closer*

to the set, taps a pensive RIZZO. RIZZO looks back, then returns attention to set.)

FELICIA
(whispering)
Is he okay?

RIZZO
Can you keep it down?

FELICIA
He's so hard on himself.

RIZZO
Why did you bring all of these people? If Nick is nervous, it's because you brought all of these goddamn people to a private production.

FELICIA
These are not people, Rizzo. These are your neighbors. And they're here because they care.

(Back on set, in front of wall cluttered with rifles, NICK swings arms, rolls neck.)

NICK
Hi, I'm Nick.
I am Nick.
Hi, I am Nick Rizzo.
I am or I'm?

Hi sounds a bit informal.

Hi, hello?

Hello, I am Nick Rizzo.

Hi, hello, hi.

Should I do Nicholas? Hi, I am Nicholas Rizzo.

*(NICK, hands in pockets, smiling. There follows an
unnerving stretch of silence. NICK remains in front of
wall, but his smile fades, replaced by a glazed stare.
He fidgets. He moves his mouth, rehearsing to himself.
Repeats: unique New York, unique New York. Repeats: how
now brown cow, how now brown cow. Off camera, a smatter
of voices. NICK turns, stares at wall of rifles. His head
moves as if he speaks to the wall. Voices off camera
increase in volume. NICK turns back to camera. Voices
quiet. He rubs eyes with back of hand and then smiles.)*

                        NICK

Hi, I'm Nick Rizzo, owner of Rizzo's Firearms. Located
just off Cave Creek and the 101, we're a family-owned
firearm retailer with an affordable yet rare selection
of weapons and accessories. However, what separates us
from every other firearm retailer in the desert is our
commitment to combatting opioid addiction. Every time
you buy a gun from us, we'll donate a percentage of
the sale to a local rehab center, halfway house, or NA
chapter. As a recovering heroin addict myself, I feel
grateful just to be here, talking. That's right: I
might have never taken a breath again. But I came back
to life, and now I'm here. In front of you. In a gun
shop.

(Pacing, NICK. Walks left, no expression, disappears. Appears walking right, mumbling, disappears. Appears walking left, pauses, holds up finger as if about to speak— voices off camera stop—then shakes head, disappears from frame. Everyone seems too ashamed to intervene. Suddenly, back on camera, NICK pauses in front of wall. His eyes are red and teary, but he smiles. He has arrived at the very beginning.)

                         NICK

   My father, David Rizzo, has made it his mission to be
   the first gun shop in America that aims for a social
   good. So come on in and tell us your story. At Rizzo's
   Firearms, we are shooting addiction dead.
   I'm sorry.
   I don't know why I'm crying. I'm not even sad.

(RIZZO, on set, in front of wall of rifles, has hands on shoulders of NICK. They remain still. NICK shoves a hand through his hair, closing his eyes.)

                        RIZZO
        (whispering)
   You're a goddamn Rizzo, Nick. Do you understand?
   You're not like all of these other fucking losers,
   okay? This place is ours. This is about destiny, kid.
   You're a Rizzo. That means something.

                         NICK

   So what? I'm a Rizzo. Who cares? What does that
   mean?

                            RIZZO

It means, well—it can mean whatever you fucking want
it to mean! Now listen up. You can do this. You have
to do this. We've got about thirty minutes left for
you to do this before we get charged for running over,
okay? Just say your lines, Nick.

*(NICK stares down. He looks as if he has just learned of
a new defeat. Then he lifts his shoulders as he inhales,
eyes closed. He exhales through his mouth.)*

                            NICK

Opioid addiction is an issue that hits home for us at
Rizzo's Firearms. I am a recovering heroin addict.
In fact, I nearly lost my life to my addiction.
Or technically I did. Lose my life. I was dead.
Technically. Actually. I had no pulse, no heartbeat.
This happens a lot. People die and then, you know.
Come back. I overdosed and died and for some reason
I came back to life. I don't know why. My skull felt
like it had been squeezed through a tube. I felt so
sorry. Not for something specific. I waited to hear a
voice, something that told me what to do, but all I
heard was myself breathing.

*(Nick stares at the camera. He tries to smile, but he
seems to be stuck in a painful flinch.)*

                            NICK

Opioid addiction is our country's most urgent issue,
and I know that because I, personally, have struggled

with heroin. And I'm here to tell you that with your
purchases, with your donations, with your money, we
can help those struggling with addiction to begin
recovery so that they can feel, so that they can start
to feel, so that the world begins to seem more—not more
manageable, but more—not less terrifying, but more—not
less boring, but more. I don't know. I just want to say
there's hope. I want to be an example of hope. But look
at me. Does this look hopeful? Do I seem recovered?
I can't do this. I'm sorry but I can't do this. Listen
to me. Look at me. I'm a loser. I'm an idiot. I died,
and I came back to life, and all I have to say is here
come buy a gun from me? This is stupid, and I can't
even fucking do it right.

*(RIZZO, now next to the camera operator, stands with his
arms crossed. In front of wall of rifles, NICK continues.)*

I practiced a lot. In the garage, in the bathroom, in
the yard, in the car. I have it all down. I just want
it to be perfect. What else do you want from me? I
said I was sorry. Dad, you're staring at me like I'm
trying to waste everyone's time.

*(Most of the crowd is gone. In front of wall of rifles,
NICK swings both hands, yelling.)*

Why don't you do it then, Dad? Yeah, if it's so easy
to stand here and tell the world that you're a junkie
piece of shit who died and came back to life then why
don't you do it? I want you to stand here, in front of

all of these stupid fucking guns, and tell everyone in
Arizona about me. I'm done.

*(RIZZO, in a pearl-snap shirt, paces off set. He runs his
ring hand through the gray curls at the back of his head
while he walks. Pauses. Bites lip. Raises a finger.)*

                         RIZZO
I'll just say my son died. I'll say something like:
opioid addiction hits home for us at Rizzo's Firearms
because my son died from heroin. That's true. That is
a true sentence. All right? Okay? What's everybody so
down about? He's fine. Just ignore him. Always been a
whiner. Always. Weak, stubborn. Always. Zero backbone.
Zero resiliency. I can see him from here. He's out in
the parking lot smoking. He wants us all to look at
him and to feel bad for him and listen to him bitch
about how hard it is to not use a drug that millions
of us have no interest in. Ignore him, I said. This
is what he has done since he was five years old. He's
thirty now, okay. Thirty.
          (Squinting. Palm to head.)
Hold on. Wait a second. Is he? Can you see if he's? My
car. My Cadillac. Where are my keys? He's getting in
my Cadillac. Wait. Jesus Christ. Hold on. Wait!

*(In front of wall of rifles, RIZZO and NICK. RIZZO's left
eye socket is pink. His right cheek is swollen. NICK
stares at the camera, no expression, a fat bottom lip,
some dried blood around his nose. RIZZO pats his frizzed
hair with both hands. NICK gestures as if trying to*

explain something, looks at his father, then looks back
above camera, hands sinking.)

RIZZO

We need to start over.

NICK

You need makeup. Can someone here do makeup?

RIZZO

Let's do a test run. A rehearsal.

NICK

Can someone help? Anyone? Please. Makeup?

RIZZO

Back to the top.

(They stand shoulder to shoulder. Father and son. They
are waiting for the signal. The scene speeds ahead: they
turn and talk and both nod to someone off set before
RIZZO puts his hands on NICK's shoulders and the two
huddle before each again turns to face the camera, which
is when—
    The scene speeds back: the men turn toward each other
and RIZZO's arms are on NICK's shoulders and then RIZZO
turns away and they both nod to—
    The scene stops. They turn toward each other. RIZZO
reaches out his arms toward his son. Pause.)

15

There was still, for Rizzo, the question of God. He was raised in the church. Roman Catholic. But his was an unpolished faith. He never managed to learn the sung refrains, instead offered what he hoped to be sonorous mumbles. Yet church was still where as an adult Rizzo found himself on Sunday mornings, until, that is, he faded from the order, subdued with shame to be alone by law. After the divorce: no confession, no alms, no sacrament, no doorway handshakes.

The day after the ad was edited, Rizzo arrived to Holy Apostles two minutes late for mass. He turned to give Nick the pick-up-the-pace gesture—rapid finger circles—as they made their way across the tiled entrance, past the raised copper bowl, the statue of Mother Mary, through the smoky smell of incense, into the room of full pews. Rizzo was struck by the attention directed toward the priest as he took his chair on the chancel. Whispers, creaking wood. "Night in Columbus?" Rizzo said to the man who led them to the back of the church, where a pair of folding chairs were beneath a crucifix.

Throughout the next fifty or so minutes father and son remained seated together, but Rizzo alone shuffled in line for communion. When had he last waited in such a line? He marched in silence with utter strangers. Drifting down the carpeted decline, toward the altar, the organ in a bellow, the stained-glass light. Rows of sunken candles burned. A man in an emerald robe stood with a chalice and gold bowl, prepared to set a quarter-sized piece of bread on the slope of each offered tongue. There came from the pews a sense of humbled restoration.

Rizzo did not believe God meddled in the success of a gun shop, though he was tempted to praise something when, on the first weekend after the ad premiered, he arrived to find people weaving from the counter all the way back to the door. He thought there was a problem. Strangers stood together under the rifles. Nick, at the front, behind the counter, raised a carbine toward a group of men with goatees. The line wound between aisles, people shuffled sideways to pull bullets from the shelves. A woman with a silver beehive split a group with smiled apologies to snatch a box of wadcutters. Behind Rizzo the door opened again. He stared into elderly faces wrapped in sunglasses. It was tough to believe: here inside Rizzo's Firearms, for the first time since the place had opened, there was a wait.

No one who spoke to Rizzo that day failed to mention the advertisement. They had caught his performance during a break in the local news or reposted somewhere online. They told him because they wanted Rizzo to know why they were here. Their son had been the homecoming king at his high school, they said, and in the summer before he was to move into his dorm at ASU, his body was found spread over a crosswalk in the Banner Health parking lot. His blue, airless, beautiful body: drugged and dumped from a still-moving Ford. And their daughter always had some problems, sure, but imagine their surprise when, after they had not heard from her in months—she had been involved with another man who was no different from the rest: older, impatient, uneducated, eager to talk of his family money—they got a collect call from a jail in Texas, then the long eighteen-hour drive through spare sweeps of earth, only to post bail and see their tall daughter wander through the steel door, their sorry Sally, easily six months pregnant. And their mother had just taken the pills her doctor had prescribed. Same with their father. Even they themselves had just done what their PCPs, their chiropractors, their dentists had said. And then, and then. Breaking into parked cars at midnight, grasping for spare change. Acrobatics over the barbed wire of junkyards. In the violent space beneath a freeway. On the curbstone, head sunk between knees, vomiting up yesterday. These were their neighbors, college roommates, parents of their kids' friends. They knew this was supposedly a disease, addiction, but you must believe them when they said they could not find any evidence of it. Often they were people who possessed very little need but plenty of want. They were lawyers, doctors, contractors, real-estate agents, owners of bridal dress shops. They were aware of how common their stories were, acknowledged this to Rizzo, and their awareness changed nothing. They prayed, prayed again, hoped and hoped. Some moved on. Their lives formed a dense shell of indifference. They disowned husbands, sons, daughters, aunts. They waited when they understood waiting was hopeless. Then they saw Rizzo's ad. They knew it was not much, but they wanted to do something, anything. Here was a chance. They felt compelled to visit. They wanted to do good, they said, but settled for what was better than nothing.

16

Spring in the valley. Miles of saguaro shadows. The mornings filled with sunlight, at night the sky the texture of avocado skin. Quails took off from the amber land. Javelinas trotted in packs. Rain stole a whole day: knuckled clouds, dark and intent, beat down on the earth—water streaking from ridges, dripping from sharp rock to sharp rock, the black paths of new mud. By the next sunrise not a single puddle remained.

Rizzo was making money. He bought a pair of cowboy boots in burgundy leather. He bought a gold ring with a square black stone. He bought a Harley with high handlebars and all-chrome fenders. (He was too scared to ride the bike on freeways and main roads, though, so in his bulky helmet he stuck to turnoffs and neighborhoods, rumbling past the ends of driveways.) He visited Cadillac dealerships, he was considering a hybrid. He was careless at the grocery store, passing up generic brands for the bold names. He took Nick out to a steakhouse and handed the waiter his card without first scrutinizing the bill for error. He felt significant. The feeling was new, insatiable, inspiring. Like the first feel of sex. To think of anything else seemed foolish. He was in demand, asked to conferences, brunches, annual fundraisers, outdoor weddings, even the funeral for a relative of Reagan.

The first talk was for the Rotary Club of Glendale. Topic? The business case for a cause: why giving profits away can bring in real returns. Rizzo let Nick take that one. On an uneven stage inside the Prickly Pear Ballroom of the DoubleTree Resort, Rizzo tried to smile as he listened to his son give *uhs* and *likes* through a speech that raised more questions than it answered. "So," Nick said, in conclusion. "Consumers want to know that their purchase, like, means something."

There was the monthly pancake breakfast for the Tempe chapter of the NRA, Friends of Firearms. It was the event Rizzo was most excited for, which made it that much more devastating when, after a speech received with thorough applause—he was there to talk about the five musts of the gun business: accuracy, activity, candor, inventory, and accounting—he found the vultures of the NRA had left nothing except scraps from a few burned pancakes.

There was the shooting range Hawaiian barbeque hosted by the Knights of Columbus from Mesa's St. John's, then the Young Republicans of Scottsdale Community College's Ice Cream Social; in partnership with the Salt River Al-Anon-/Alateen Program, the National Law Enforcement Firearms Instructors Association sponsored a rodeo at the Cave Creek Memorial Arena, inviting Rizzo and Nick to the center of the corral, where they received a boot-shaped plaque for Cowboy Excellence. Nick reached for the mic before Rizzo and, after a period of his expected bungling, delivered the rousing gun shop slogan: aim for more!

But the sign that Rizzo entered a higher social stratum came when Bill Friar, of Friar Lighting, asked that Rizzo appear in Queen Creek at a warehouse to cut the ribbon for a grand reopening.

"Morals are big," Bill Friar said. He wore a pair of aviators and was dressed like a Franciscan monk. A much shorter woman tried to apply foundation to his neck without having her hand struck by the end of Bill's bobbing cigar. They were in a shadowed corner of the strip mall—Bill, Rizzo, Nick, a few others—while nearby a member of the production crew unwound a bundle of wires. A modest crowd, phones out, formed behind the cordoned sidewalk.

"I'm interested in a collaboration," said Tony Tomayaki, who, after patting Bill on the shoulder, had introduced himself to Rizzo with a baffling sincerity. Tony owned the Toyota dealership where Rizzo once worked, but luckily seemed to not remember when, during one of Tony's rare but consequential visits to the sales floor, Rizzo reversed a Tundra over the foot of a customer. "Guns and cars," Tony said, shaking a finger. "These belong to the desert." A comment that inspired Nick to deliver a spirited monologue about their shared principles of design.

"That's what's missing from this country. Specialization," said Doug Halston, a local congressman with a wet comb-over. "Did anyone ever ask him in school if he wanted to be a plumber?" He pointed at Nick. "It's a subject I'm hoping to address through state testing."

They prepared for photos behind the red tape; looking from camera to camera, Rizzo smiled hard enough to hurt his face.

But victory, and all of its associated praise, was an isolating experience, Rizzo learned. People he had never liked anyway were being bought out by the man he had spurned, Buford Bellum. Anticipating them gone, Rizzo felt a sudden longing for his neighbors.

"He told me that being an entrepreneur is like being a great fighter: you've got to know when to walk away," said Dante Bowers, the owner of the corner unit, a tae kwon do studio, when he invited himself to join Rizzo for a smoke break on the sidewalk. Dante was dressed in his ribbed gi and black belt, barefoot, a six-pack of Keystone under an arm. "Once the sale goes through, I'm moving to Jamaica," Dante said. "Jamaica or Hawaii. I want to live in a place where I can run on the beach."

Rizzo imagined a jogging Dante on a beach of cool sand, above the fizzing tide—there went his neighbor, delighted on the shoreline. Enjoy it, Dante! May the seaweed be sparse.

"He towered over my husband, and you know how tall Ryan is," said Cassandra Martinez, the owner of Mountain Peak Nutrition, when she walked over to Rizzo's Cadillac's driver-side window to ramble for half an hour. Sitting there in his idling car with both hands on the wheel, Rizzo watched Cassandra speak with such excitement that, beneath her platinum blond bob, a vein popped from her neck down across her muscular shoulders. "We're going to retire up north with the money," Cassandra told Rizzo. "We found a cabin with the best views."

A polygonal cabin—Rizzo could see it: the competing peaks of a log-lined roof, glass walls on the first floor, and on the wraparound deck, facing the sullen white woods, Cassandra and Ryan sat bundled before a fire, their expressions content in the flames.

"He's one of the few people left who does business the right way," said Brent Pollian, as if Rizzo had asked. Brent owned Healed Hogs, the motorcycle repair shop—and he had wandered over from the dumpster, invading the otherwise serene area out back where Rizzo sat in his usual spot staring out at the transmission towers. There was a sunset of purple beams. "And anyway," Brent said, smacking Rizzo on the shoulder, "now that I can get out of debt? I'm going to buy a Cessna. I've always wanted to fly to Milwaukee."

He was fine with Brent gone. Please, take him! He saw the jovial Brent in a leather jacket, in the cockpit of a sleek plane, falling toward the ground.

Most of all, Rizzo felt a sadness at the prospect of no more Felicia. He wanted to ask for more lemons—not because he needed them, but because he liked the idea of her thinking of him, of her sparing the fruit from her home.

17

Hey, it's Rizzo. Give me a call back. Talk soon.

—

Hey, Rizzo again. Okay. Thanks.

—

You're going to laugh your ass off when you hear Brent's plan to buy an airplane. This guy's a pilot? He can't tie his shoes correctly. When he's in the air, I'll be underground.

—

What do you think about a partnership? People who come into Rizzo's Firearms get a discount at Southwest Pool Stuff. Or something. Nick wants to talk, too. He wants to help with some digital stuff. I've got him working on a website for you. All right. Call me back.

—

Is this about the ad? About when we were filming and I was, well, maybe a bit short with you? Is that it? Because if so, I was pissed at Nick. I didn't mean to take it out on you.

—

Or is this about Buford? If so, you should've heard how he was talking to me. Was I supposed to sit there and take that? To sit there and be humiliated? The first time, with me missing the meeting—look, I take responsibility, even though that was Nick's fault. But when I saw him at the Waffle House—I mean, come on. Am I not allowed to have self-respect? Am I supposed to smile as I'm shat upon by Mr. Big Time?

—

I thought more about it and I can see how, in your situation, after you went out of your way to help me—not once but twice—you might therefore be frustrated. And for that I am sorry. You're my friend, and I care about you, so that's why I've been calling. And I don't mean that I care about you in a weird way. I don't have many friends, Felicia. That's not a complaint. I'm satisfied with my social circle. It's a very narrow circle. So narrow it might just be considered a dot. But you are contained within my social dot for a reason, and the reason is that I care about you in a normal and acceptable and friendly—

18

Rizzo, leaning against the door of Southwest Pool Stuff, decided that Felicia had died; oh, yes: suddenly, violently. What else? He imagined being notified of her expiration through a terse email, then asked to clean out her shop. Rizzo, in mourning, shoving foam noodles in black trash bags.

But soon her lifted Wrangler parked in a spot that should have gone to a customer.

"They wanted me to claim her body, even though I haven't talked to my kid in five years," Felicia said. They were inside her shop, near the register, and Rizzo watched as she patiently tore open an envelope. Light came through the tinted windows in waves. "Seven-hour drive to Ephraim," Felicia said. "Utah. Who knows what she was doing there. Well, actually, not hard to figure out. After all, overdose. Guy she used with was in the morgue. Boyfriend or whatever. Crying like he loved her. Bony bastard with a hat, smearing his face with a bandana, shrieking like a little girl. Disgusting. I hugged him. Can you believe that?" She stared at Rizzo. "I looked at him and thought, This is someone's child. It was disgusting. Afterward I was in the parking lot dry heaving. I thought it would make me feel better, but I guess I didn't have anything in me."

Rizzo was next to an overgrown bamboo tree, unsure, embarrassed. He wanted to shrink behind the leaves. "I'm sorry," he said, and immediately regretted saying. He stared at the ground, feeling like an idiot. Eager to leave, he was anxious to not seem impolite.

Felicia flipped through the rest of the mail, dropping envelopes in the garbage. "I have to ask," she said. "With Nick. How does it feel?"

"Feel?"

"He's still here. Alive."

"Right," Rizzo said. "I'm very lucky. I pray to God every day. I used to ask for things. Now I just say thanks."

Felicia pulled her hair back, staring at the floor. "I talked to Buford," she said. "I'll be out at the end of the month."

When Rizzo left the shop that day he thought of Felicia in a parking lot in central Utah, all alone, failing to expel that awful grief from her body.

Not long after she got into an argument with a customer over a parking spot. Both hands in the air, she yelled at the hood of a truck: "What are you going to do? Shoot me? Oh, that would just be fantastic!" Rizzo hustled out once he heard the car horns—but had his hand slapped away from Felicia's shoulder. She pointed a finger. "Don't touch me," she said, before shoving past him.

It was maybe a week later when a customer in a white cowboy hat came up to Rizzo, smiling. "They'll protest anything now," he said, nodding toward the window.

A triple-digit day—the heat visible: flickering spirals—but there was Felicia, in a corner of the business park, holding a sign. She was dressed as if on her way to play tennis: white visor, tank top, leggings. GUN OWNERS KILL CHILDREN, her sign said. Cars honked. There were shouts from Felicia, shouts from customers. Rizzo, watching, with an impressive amount of agita, outside before he thought of what to say.

"What the fuck, Felicia?" He stepped onto the curb. "What the hell is this about?"

Felicia stood from her chair, raised her sign. "This is about the blood on the hands of all gun owners in America. This is about the murdered children all American gun owners need to answer for. This is about the terror that gun owners bring upon schools and malls and churches all across America—the *terrorism* that gun owners perpetuate every day. This is about how your selfishness—your stupid hobby"—here she pointed at Rizzo, still yelling, "leads to the slaughter of children."

"Jesus Christ—okay, okay, okay." Rizzo, whispering with his hands out, glanced from Felicia back to the customers walking in and out of his shop.

"I've overlooked so many things," Felicia said, softer. She was talking to Rizzo but looking away. "I've always believed there was a right way to live. It's simple. Right, wrong. But then I excuse people. I compromise, I pretend not to care, I move on. Like that kid who was with my daughter. And like with you, Rizzo. I've always hated guns. I've always told you I hated guns, but I kept acting as if you—as my friend, as a person—should for some reason not be judged for doing wrong. But you should. You all should."

Shame settled across Rizzo's face and turned to an anger that tightened his shoulders as he walked away from Felicia, the shouting nutjob whom he mistook for his only friend. Rizzo smiled wildly at every last face he encountered inside his shop while his heart melted between his lungs.

Sorry, but did he invent the handgun? Ever since Rizzo got out of the Army he had been wandering around with his head bowed, begging to be kicked in the balls if it meant he would have enough money to be recognized as a decent citizen—but Felicia said he was the bad guy! Because Rizzo decided the interest rates on his son's student loans meant that he needed to work himself to dust! Because Rizzo was the rich motherfucker with a five-thousand-square-foot stucco bungalow in Arcadia with a diving board above his heated pool!

Here was a question: If Rizzo did what was *right*, if he went ahead and donated all of his guns to ISIS so that they could blow our heads off, then would Felicia pay his mortgage? Oh, she wouldn't? Well, let him see here, since he was now almost sixty and, before he opened his own business, got fired from his last three sales jobs for missing his Q4 quotas—even though he would've hit his number at West Valley Hyundai if his goddamn boss would've budged on the discount for those tires; hell, he would've been first in the President's Club at Chupacabra Honda if Enrique Gomez had not recruited every last fucking aunt of his to buy a Civic!—but, if he lost his business, then would Felicia give him a job? Oh, but that's right, she sold? Would she let him live in her house? Ah. Okay. Understood. Of course, of course. Well, in that case, maybe you could do Rizzo a favor and, if you don't mind, go right on ahead and fuck yourself!

Not that Rizzo said any of this. What would have been the point? He could not shake the sense that he was the one somehow wrong.

"It's great for business," Nick said, as he swiped the credit card of a woman with a blond mullet buying a dozen boxes of .22 shells. Rizzo, on a stool, had his face in his hands. "Gun owners?" Nick whispered, motioning toward the next in line. "They want to have an enemy, Dad. They want to feel like everyone is against them. Great. You should hope she sits out there every day. Actually, you should pay her to sit out there every day."

It did not take long for Rizzo to be back at the window, despondent, as the customers took pictures, recorded videos, whatever. He thought Felicia would wilt in the heat. Wrong. She waved the sign like a flag.

A half dozen men gathered, most large and white. Some were bald, bearded, many were overweight, the sort of men you could imagine in cubicles waiting for their phones to ring. A few wore camo hats, others were in tank tops, often the sides of their heads were buzzed. After an exchange Rizzo could not hear through the window, he watched as Felicia picked up the bowls of cat food and began throwing handfuls of kibble at the group.

"Murderers, sickos, whackos, fuckheads." She was composed in her speech, Rizzo noticed, as he made his way through the crowd. She was throwing the food overhand. She began a chant: "Tiny. Dick. Cowards. Tiny. Dick. Cowards. Tiny. Dick. Cowards." Which provoked little more than some laughs and a few muffled calls.

Rizzo made it to the front of the crowd just in time to be hit in the eye with Felicia's spit. Had that been meant for him? He wiped his face, then stood there, stunned, while the noise rose from those assembled.

19

On an otherwise unremarkable Wednesday at Sunnyside High School, an assault rifle fired more than two hundred rounds in the cafeteria, across the halls, inside the cramped classrooms. Because of the exceptional muzzle velocity, 325-grain hollow-point bullets were dispensed from the weapon at about twice the speed of sound.

The local networks replayed aerial footage of the evacuation. Muted, kids wandered from a school building, their arms raised in horror. They were beneath the portico attached to the massive complex of tan concrete, and they moved beside the copper statue, past the armored Hummer parked at a rushed angle, the officers in full body armor holding their rifles at rest. There was sun on corrugated steel, alarm lights. Clouds over the mountains. The officers motioned at the lines of children to hurry up, keep moving, let's go. All the kids seemed about the same size. Some stuck their hands higher as they neared the officers, then took off sprinting through the parking lot. A few needed help. One boy, in particular, who limped not from a wound but from the force of his crying, and the girl who lugged his backpack over her shoulder, who yanked him along with her own arms. She stuck her hands high at the sight of an approaching officer. The boy had no choice but to fall down in the yellow grass. The others stepped over and around the fallen, and then, all over again, the expected replay: kids, in orderly rows, pouring from the building.

In a first for the short but prolific history of American school shootings, not a single person was killed, and no student nor teacher was injured. The shooter even spared himself, surrendering next to a poster in the cafeteria that detailed the Heimlich. This was how the police found him: facedown in the cafeteria, his hands behind his head, weeping. Oh, the school building was destroyed—walls were caverned, desks and chairs and computer monitors disintegrated. Brick ash coated the floors. In the footage of reporters outside the school, classroom lights stayed on into the night.

Many wondered what force was responsible for the improbable converging: for this uncoordinated boy, in possession of a powerful weapon, to miss that much? To reload? To reload again? It was concluded that the gun, a .50-caliber Beowulf, built for an experienced shooter, had been too much for the aspiring murderer. Mr. Alvarez, an economics teacher who shielded students with his own body, described the boy being overtaken by the gun, how he struggled even to hold the frantic object. "I couldn't shut my eyes," Mr. Alvarez said.

Rizzo watched coverage of the shooting in a post-dinner recline. In the kitchen Nick bagged sandwiches for the next day's lunch. The broadcaster named the gun again. Beowulf, the broadcaster said—and that was when Rizzo sat up.

20

Arizona gun dealer arrested for supplying weapon to mass shooter

By Randy Rocha, CNN

Updated 2:50 PM EST, Wed April 23, 2014

Phoenix (CNN)—In what was a surprise to no one, the owner of Rizzo's Firearms, David A. Rizzo, was denied bail at his preliminary hearing this morning. Mr. Rizzo allegedly sold a .50 caliber assault rifle to the seventeen-year-old Sunnyside High School mass shooter, Steven Ruck, who is awaiting sentencing after pleading guilty to attempted murder. (The event has **been called** "The Mass Survival.") In the state of Arizona, no one under the age of eighteen is allowed to purchase a firearm . . .

SECOND AMENDMENT | Published April 23, 2014, 2:51 PM EDT

Up in Arms: American hero controversially denied bail

Lawyer says Arizona small business owner and philanthropist the scapegoat

By Hannah Bladin | Fox News

While Mr. Rizzo's lawyer, Mundo Rodriguez, claims the decision to deny bail is "outrageous" and that his client executed the necessary steps per Arizona's state law before selling Mr. Ruck the Beowulf. Mr. Rodriguez said that the shooter provided false identification and questioned whether Mr. Ruck should be considered a mass shooter when he did not shoot a single person, **a point many have raised**. The attorney for Mr. Rizzo went on to say that his

client is receiving an unfair judicial process because of two of the survivors'
connections to high-ranking state government officials.

Mr. Rodriguez was referring to Arizona Supreme Court Justice Fred Lillian, a
three-term judge perhaps best known for his decision in *Julian vs. Honey Dip
Fro-Yo*, in which Justice Lillian, citing *Citizens United*, ruled that a company
may express its own sexual inclinations in the same legally appropriate manner
as an individual citizen, a decision that those on the far left have said **enables
workplace harassment**; and Senator Beatrice Sid, a first-term Republican
senator who **gained notoriety** for her innovative campaign calendar which
featured photos of her topless with an AR-15. Justice Lillian's daughter, Lainey,
and Senator Sid's son, Bill, were both present on the day of the Sunnyside
High School shooting.

yahoo!news

THE WASHINGTON POST

"Justice Begins Today": the survivors would like a word

Frances Orb

Weds, April 23, 2014, at 2:52 PM

Survivors and their families overwhelmingly agreed with the decision by
the prosecuting attorney, Brianna Stephanos. Ms. Stephanos explained that
although the defendant faces no higher than a Class 4 felony, his "celebrity
status in the gun-owner community makes (Mr. Rizzo) an obvious risk to
receive far-reaching aid to flee trial." Ms. Stephanos also cited the video Mr.
Ruck posted on Facebook prior to entering the school—in which he is recorded
saying, "My life is meaningless. I have no purpose. I want everyone to feel the
same way I do"—as establishing the intent of a mass murderer and justifying
the charges against Mr. Rizzo. Thus far Mr. Rizzo has been charged with illegal
sale of a firearm, fraud and attempted involuntary manslaughter.

NBC NEWS | MASS SHOOTINGS

David Rizzo became a star to those in the gun and recovery communities. Some question whether he was ever deserving of praise.

The man many believed popularized the idea of the "mission-based weapons dealer" comes under fire

4/23/2014, 2:53 PM EDT

By Greg Hart

Mr. Rizzo became a community hero after his advertisement for his gun shop, which aired on local television, went viral. The advertisement, included above, shows Mr. Rizzo with his son, Nick, a recovering heroin addict who claims to have overdosed and died before being resuscitated with Naloxone by the staff at Phoenix's Banner Health. Naloxone is a nasal spray often administered to those experiencing respiratory depression from opioid use.

In the advertisement, Mr. Rizzo and his son claim that a percentage of all sales will be donated to organizations throughout the Phoenix area committed to "shooting addiction dead." The ad sparked debate online about whether a firearm retailer or any other business that sells controversial products should be able to benefit financially from its philanthropy. However, citing Rizzo's Firearms's pledge as inspiration, several small businesses across the country have come up with causes of their own. Mesa's Mother Vaper released an advertisement in solidarity with Rizzo's Firearms and said a percentage of all of its profits would be donated to groups committed to "looking into pulmonary issues and stuff."

Nick Rizzo, part owner of Rizzo's Firearms, said he was "more than willing to talk to the press." When reached for comment, Nick only repeated that he "did not know what to say."

21

"Racially, tensions are high right now," Rizzo said, "but I'm well cared for."
He was in an orange jumpsuit, leaning toward the glass. "The one in St.
Louis? What he smoked a cigar so they shot him? We're not allowed to
watch the news. They're worried about a riot. It's not so much between
prisoners, but the guards and the Black prisoners—that's where tensions
are high. The guards want to squash a riot early. Problem is, there's no
riot planning per se that I can tell, so the guards are just beating the shit
out of any Black guy they think might want to start a riot. Which I'm
pretty confident will inspire these guys to start planning an actual riot."

Nick, with a slouch, in need of a shave, softly: "But are you eating?"

"It's kind of like being in the military," Rizzo said, to the ceiling.
"Group of miserable guys with lots of rules who mostly find a way to
entertain themselves. Except I'm only supposed to talk to white guys
over the age of fifty. Not to mention the amenities. You know how I get
water to drink in my cell? Toilet. Only water available to drink is from
the toilet. Well, I deserve it." Low, amazed, to himself: "They all said I'm
lucky I got a deal. If I was convicted of everything I'd spend the next
twenty years in this place." Looking up at Nick: "You know where I'll
be in twenty years? Dead, that's where."

"Don't cry, Dad."

After some time, muffled: "Everyone survived. A miracle. And I
wanted a sign? I was supposed to be done with guns. Now I'm a felon,

I'll never be able to own a gun again." Rizzo looked up at his son. "There's something bigger than me, bigger than you, bigger than that little dipshit who tried to kill everyone."

"What do you mean?"

"I mean go do your marketing thing. Sell the business, keep the house. Please, don't lose the house. When I get out of here, I'll figure out something."

"I'm sorry but . . ."

"Hold the phone closer to your mouth Nick," rubbing his nose. "I can't hear a thing you're saying."

"I said I'm—"

"Well not that close. Jesus Christ you just put a prison phone in your mouth."

"Dad, wait till you see what I do with the place. We'll have a booth at every weapons expo across the country. By the time you get out of here, we'll have four locations, fifty full-time employees, a marketing department. We'll be doing ten million a month. We'll have billboards, a fully optimized website. I'll own the competition by the time you're out of here, Dad. I mean literally own. I'll buy them out."

"No, Nick. Listen. I don't want any of that."

"I'm sorry, Dad. I'm sorry you're in here."

"No I mean Nick all I want is for you to be—"

"Dad: I know, I know, I know."

—

He flashes on. His face has a slight tan compared to his neck, he's smiling, but his cheer becomes strange when registered with his surroundings: mounted shotguns and long-barrel rifles form the backdrop, striking both in their form and their abundance. A second man swings himself into the frame. His cowboy boots give off more of a shine than his jewelry. He introduces himself with a startling confidence.

There is a sense of their relation from looks alone. It's in the eyes, it's in the nose, it's in the identical desperation with which they both hold their shoulders. But it's also in how they end a vowel.

They give statements about the inventory. There's an acknowledgment of the crisis in the desert. Opioids. Our duty to each other, the younger man says, is as essential to America as our right to bear arms. They conclude with a bout of overlapping speech. Come on down. They hold their pose. It is a portrait. It is a hard promise. The father with a hand on the shoulder of his son.

II

2017

1

Used, yes. A glass tower filled with used hybrids. It was known as the Eiffel Tower Dealership. No salesmen needed. Buttons were pressed, steel levers engaged. A sought vehicle lowered. It was the highest building south of the lake, a shard on the edge of the desert town, closer to those square neighborhoods below than any of the spiking mountains. Across the four-lane boulevard, Nick Rizzo stood outside a church of old white stucco, admiring the structure. He wore a gray company shirt. His curly hair was uncombed. He was barely overweight. Because he had lost his sunglasses, he stared up with a squint and a smile at the transparent boxes, finding the cars suitably apocalyptic.

Through the propped doors of the church came a fading antiphon. Soon those parishioners who skipped out right after the eucharist became a colorful march from the shade of the building to a table of yellow flyers, to another table with warm coffee and jelly doughnuts, and then the sprawl of guns.

A man in a collared shirt and sneakers turned over a Glock in his hands. "Does this shoot underwater?" he wanted to know. "Or what if I drop it in water," the man said. "I drop it in my pool. Then pick it up. Will it shoot?"

Oh, Nick Rizzo said, it will shoot: the Glock could fire through the blinding winds of a haboob—and then he swiped the man's credit card through the plastic square that attached to the tablet.

"Bobcats." A woman with rings on all ten fingers was holding a

Beretta shotgun up from the table. "Will it be enough for bobcats?" Now she held up a Bushmaster.

Bobcats were nothing, Nick Rizzo said: the Bushmaster could put down rhinoceroses, elephants, vultures, any stratospheric objects—pausing in his list to lick the fingertip he used for cash counting, he swiped each bill from the stack the woman handed over.

"Hi there sonny. Do you happen to know if this thing here can pierce a military tank?" A man with silver hair combed into an oval asked this. He had on high socks and khaki shorts and his button-down was made of material intended to disguise sweat. In his hands was a .458 SOCOM, a sizable rifle that would fracture his sternum with its recoil. "I'm building a bunker up north," the man explained. "Me and my fourth wife, we're hiding out there." He told Nick it was because of the crisis at the border, the Antifa, the BLMers, also the CIA and the FBI, plus the National Guard—so he was staying up north until Trump cooled things down, drained the swamp. "So, what do you think," the man said.

What Nick thought was that the .458 came to just under three thousand dollars.

But the man was not done. "It gives me hope to meet young people like yourself," he said. He stood there cradling his new rifle. His name was Roger McDuffie and he believed the world had ended years ago. "This is the afterlife of civilization," Roger said. Nick tried to disengage, but after each attempt Roger spoke louder. He said corporations had surreptitiously replaced our souls with algorithms. He said the family as an institution had been transmogrified into a loveless focus group. The education system, he said, had left our youth in perpetual spiritual mourning. "But every once in a while I meet someone like you," Roger told Nick, "someone who reminds me of myself, and I think maybe, after the incalculable amounts of imminent bloodshed, after the race wars, and the chemical wars—well, maybe then there'll be a fellow with some

old-fashioned nose-to-the-pavement work ethic who'll help rebuild us."
Roger stuck out a hand. He said, "If you ever need a bunker."

The church emptied without the slightest note of ceremony. Quails,
clouds. A disconcerting amount of sunshine. The sky blared an unbroken
blue. A figure in a green robe traveled down the wavering concrete.

"My God, my God, why have you abandoned me," sang Father Bill,
as he knocked his knuckles against the side of the van. Nick shoved
the last table into the back, lit a cigarette, then handed Father Bill the
envelope of cash.

"Amen," Father Bill said, tapping the envelope against his chest.

They stood there staring out at the parking lot.

"Father Bill," Nick said, "if you disagree with everything someone
believes, can you have a relationship with that person?"

"You mean sexually," Father Bill asked, still looking straight ahead.

"I mean a business relationship."

"I'm not sure," Father Bill said, before explaining that it depended
on what, exactly, Nick was asking. A relationship in a logical sense? Sure,
why not. But in a moral sense? As in, was it morally permissible for Nick
Rizzo to do business with someone who lived in sin? Father Bill first
needed to know why Nick could judge *what* was sinful.

"For the sake of the argument," Nick said.

Then did Nick believe, Father Bill asked, that the person might
eventually repent? Accept Christ? Confess?

"No," Nick said.

It was not necessarily wrong, Father Bill concluded. As long as Nick
believed the person could be redeemed—which was what Nick should
believe, because it was what God told His Son to believe—yeah, then it
should be fine. Okay, but what if you start to become like that person?
Not to believe the same things, necessarily, Nick said, but to act in the
same way? Better put: What happens if you act in a way that you know
is wrong, but you believe in what is right? What then? Nick was under

the impression that a person was not defined by his actions, but did the Lord, like, agree?

"I'm just a priest," Father Bill said.

Soon Nick steered the Rizzo's Firearms van through Phoenix, across roads that looked wet from the strength of the light, beneath digital bill-boards flashing in the daytime sky; he passed an unpaved neighborhood that, replete with scaffolding for future homes, resembled dazzling ruins; a grimacing man stood on a median, raising water bottles at the traffic; a woman in a sweatshirt pushed a shopping cart toward tents made out of blankets and patched tarps; the green brick of the Sandman Hotel, then the purple brick of the Lamplighter Motel, around which grown men wobbled on tiny bicycles; a sign read: DRIVE HAMMERED, GET NAILED; an old meat smoker beside a stack of treadless tires; clusters of twisted pipes whistled in the power plant, the next lot over filled exclusively with forklifts; people outside a pool hall in the storefront shade, and in the parking lot, on rumbling Harleys, women wrapped their arms around their bandanaed men; condos behind a stop on the light rail, and the clanking ride of the train beneath the commanding wires, before a roundabout lined with lemon trees, then the freeway ramp that gave view to a burst of true desert: noble miles adorned with cactus; it was the time of year when many of the succulents had pink-petaled flowers pinched between their glochids.

The east valley. Bleached trails of the McDowell Mountains. Here was his next stop, a recently constructed guide center: a building with gold siding that provided shade to those preparing for or recovering from their walks. There were bathrooms, water fountains. People in white hats and black tights, stretching at the trail side. Thompson Peak rose in the distance as the victorious conclusion of the base. Shadows from the few westward clouds drifted across its radio tower.

A metal bridge led hikers above a sediment canal to the splitting trails. It was here that Nick Rizzo now stood beneath the tent with his guns for sale.

"We're offending the idea of the miraculous," said a shirtless man in a bicycle helmet, gesturing with his new .357 beneath the tent.

To which Nick Rizzo said thank you very much for your purchase.

Miles west: sunset above the low roofs of new construction. An entire world of downtown colors. Daunting clouds. Though too white to be rain clouds, Nick Rizzo thought, as he lit a needed cigarette. Racing to an appropriate climate, they were a vast country variety.

As a finishing purple stretched across the landscape, Nick turned onto the circuitous route that led to the business park. Except now along the ride, rather than anguished debris, there were competing fast-food restaurants, insurance offices, haircut franchises, a pet-grooming business painted a lurid green. Next to Rizzo's Firearms there was no more Southwest Pool Stuff, no more Mountain Peak Nutrition. Now there was a Quiznos. There was a Firestone Tire. A CVS next to a Dairy Queen next to a Sweet Salad. Out behind the business park all that could be seen of the new neighborhood was a pink wall that cut between transmission towers.

There were protestors at Rizzo's Firearms. Nick heard them before he turned onto the road that curved around the back of the complex. A decent number spread across the asphalt, with some on the curb, people with signs and shirts and misaligned chants. News crews on the borders. A man in a black hat stepped out of the gun shop, staring. From the crowd a woman in sunglasses emerged with a piece of paper in her hand. Who else? Felicia. Everyone around her bowed their heads or held up their phones.

There had been more than two hundred mass shootings so far this year, Felicia said. It was April. She listed the cities, the numbers killed and injured. Indianapolis, Indiana, she said: one dead, four injured. Detroit, Michigan: two dead, three injured. Orlando, Florida: six dead, fourteen injured. Albuquerque, New Mexico: nine injured. Rome, New York: four dead, twelve injured. Lowell, Massachusetts: two dead, six injured. Baton Rouge, Louisiana: one dead, five injured. Cypress, Texas: four dead, ten injured. New London, Connecticut: three dead, seven injured. Richmond, Virginia: one dead, six injured. Reno, Nevada: nine dead, eighteen injured. Saint Paul, Minnesota: two dead, eleven injured. Tucson, Arizona: three dead, eight injured. Eugene, Oregon: five dead, seven injured—

Something snapped in the chest of Nick Rizzo. And then an irritating heat rose in his throat. He leaned out the window and surprised himself with the force of his yell. "Hey," he shouted. "Hey! Fuck you. Yeah. You. Go fuck yourself!"

2

Rizzo's Firearms @rizzosfirearms · Apr 28
what does SIG stand for? 1st in replies gets 20% off sig sauer tread
predator #sig #rizzosfirearms

Rizzo's Firearms @rizzosfirearms · Apr 28
caught up w/ Curtis Wheat @wheatbrizzy who just hit his 90 day
milestone (link in replies) proud to donate to local rehabs and
sober houses

Rizzo's Firearms @rizzosfirearms · Apr 29
moment when dude calls hotdog "wiener" #weird #guns #bbq

Rizzo's Firearms @rizzosfirearms · Apr 29
free for subscribers live stream action at the range #bethere #hollowpoint

Rizzo's Firearms @rizzosfirearms · Apr 29
great partnership event w/ @kustomkannons and @southvalleyrange
#explodingcinderblocks

Rizzo's Firearms @rizzosfirearms · Apr 30
everyone has someone they love struggling right now w/
addiction #opioids #love #soberlivingnearme #onedayatatime
#gunownersagainstsacklers

Rizzo's Firearms @rizzosfirearms · Apr 30
next door neighbor @smoothieking giving 10% off all smoothies to any1
w/ RF swag

Rizzo's Firearms @rizzosfirearms · May 1
curious: glock still the best sidearm? #history #debate

3

How long had Nick Rizzo been sober?

Over three years, but he resisted the idea that he could be defined by the simple maintenance of his sobriety.

Who was he then?

The man who picked the buck. A fact he felt some guilt for, yes, but he believed his self-awareness spared him from being truly unprincipled. He would make the right choice when it mattered most.

What if such a choice never came?

Oh, it would.

But if not?

He still had to work. Even the infrequent afternoon off for Nick still involved hanging around the business. In his nominal absence the shop was managed by Matt Wilson, a friend from high school who had shared Nick's desire to flee Arizona. Also had, for a bit: to Southern California, almost a decade. As teenagers they often skipped P.E. to smoke cigarettes and rehearse sketches for their future auditions for *Saturday Night Live*, hiding out for the entire fourth period at Matt's house, where both boys had displayed a humor limited to the scatological, the onanistic, and Kaufmanesque anti-jokes, though neither, at the time, had any idea who Andy Kaufman was.

They had talked for the first time in years when Nick got back online. Matt Wilson had been living in his parents' garage in Glendale, answering the phone at a glassblowing studio, four years and thirte days sober. He was tall and blond and blue-eyed, naturally lean, with the slack demeanor of someone secure in his tastes. His disinterest in the age or quality of his clothes—he often wore cotton T-shirts with random slogans across the chest, with phrases like HANG LOOSE and GO AZTECS and NEVER FORGET: HAVASU '09—only further contributed to Matt's vibe of seasoned indifference.

Today Matt Wilson spoke to a man with sideburns and a checkered tie while on the glass surface between them was an antique rocket launcher. "You remember Danny," Matt said, swinging a thumb at the man with the sideburns. But Nick did not remember Danny, so Matt continued: "The real-estate agent. He's been showing a bunch of stuff for that neighborhood out back?"

"The rockets," Danny said. He swung a briefcase down on the counter next to the bazooka.

"It's supposed to be decorative," Matt said, nodding at Nick, while he struggled to unclasp the latches.

Here was a question: Did Nick believe in redemption?

It was asked by Matt when Danny left. Why did Matt need to know, was Nick's response, which received a shrug. Matt Wilson said he was trying to talk about things that mattered. He remembered attempting a vow of silence as a kid, how he briefly thought there was something profound in silence, but he realized it seemed that way because it was also a form of laziness.

Had Matt Wilson been smoking pot?

A little. Several hours earlier. "I fucked up," Matt said, staring down. This was not the first time he had fucked up. He stood at the counter and gripped the rocket launcher as if it were a rail holding him upright. "Danny came around and I just, you know, fucked up."

"It's a mistake," Nick said.

"I want to go to a meeting," Matt Wilson said. "There's this meeting in Scottsdale that this chick told me about. Let me text her real quick."

When would his father be released?

Eighteen months and a handful of days. There were moments when the time seemed insurmountable, there were moments when it seemed not enough. Visits to Florence, the prison town. He remembered the first as if it were the last. The black landline, aged by the decades. The gloss on the phone from past nervous hands. The weight of the phone in Nick's own hand. He had sat on that stiff chair—he remembered this—and found his father behind the glass. He had stared into the holes of the phone, and while he stared, his father yelled—yelled loud enough that Nick heard what was said through the phone without holding it to his ear. The colossal voice. He had known the vibrations in his hand meant the voice of his father. A beautiful thing. His father: contained, safe, of definite shape. But when he had looked back at his father, everything had changed. His suddenly shriveled father, with aged skin swollen around his eyes, the pathetically high finish of his hairline. He had studied this new man, his father, with a love so singular it produced a chilling fear. What if, what if. The hope-choked sound of his father's voice. Miracle, his father said. Miracle.

4

The desire to be seen without the fortitude to withstand judgment—here was Nick Rizzo's condition. It was acquired from his years in New York, where he found everyone gave off a fabled glare. Which meant he needed to catch up: a cream linen suit, unbuttoned in the front—purchased in SoHo. He liked the loose feel of the linen against his chest. He thought he would wear it through the cramped summer months, then on his flight for Christmas: he imagined himself stepping off the plane in Sky Harbor, luxuriously wrinkled, hustling with a duffel to nod at his waiting father. If only! Each time he had tried the thing on at home he was surprised and disappointed in his body. Not in the quality of the clothes, but in the way their quality had revealed the poor shape of himself. So the suit had stayed folded in a corner of his closet. Same with the floral button-ups and striped polos. Instead he wore neutral shades that seemed intent on their own negation.

There was one exception, which Nick wore tonight: the denim jacket, with a cream leather collar—faded near black—that once belonged to his father.

It was a full-moon night and cold for the desert. Nick typed another tweet, then looked up from his phone at those gathered nearby who, smoking, showing the occasional shiver, talked in the light from their screens. Matt Wilson was whispering in the ear of a woman with pronounced collarbones. She had on lipstick and a dress, held her one long braid in both hands. Matt had mentioned a friend to

Nick—this was how he justified asking for a ride—but no friend had yet materialized.

The NA meeting started after a karate session for children. Kids could be seen rolling across a rubberized floor, resisting their parents' attempts to remove the straps from their foot pads. The room itself was in an intricate office park that, recessed from the main thoroughfare, resembled a modern adobe castle. Restaurants with extravagant exteriors. A proud dental office, a spare antiques shop. Many on the first floor vacant, in their windows forgotten boxes from banished tenants.

It was the headlights that Nick noticed first. The convertible with long doors pulled deeper into the lot. Coupe DeVille. One of the street boats of the seventies in a celebratory white.

Buford Bellum emerged from the vehicle. It was him, Nick was sure of it, just as he was also sure that the desert tycoon had gotten a bad deal when negotiating with time: strolling toward the site of the meeting in a polished leather jacket and loafers, Buford was maybe fifty pounds heavier than Nick remembered from the billboards. Yet the man walked with a sense of defiant ownership. In fact, he seemed determined to walk right through Nick, so when he instead slowed with a hand raised, Nick could not help but feel pulled into a polite tide, and he returned the wave, smiling, calling out to Buford as if he had been a dear friend to his father.

The wave, however, had not been intended for Nick but instead for a mother departing the studio with a teary son. They all paused near Nick, the mother and son and Buford, glancing over with the requisite embarrassment on his behalf before exchanging pleasantries to one another: Buford and Cheryl had not seen each other in some time, this was her son, Billy, who had just completed his first class, say hi Billy—and as soon as they walked off, Buford turned to Nick with a thoughtful squint. Did they know each other?

"Kind of," Nick said. "Rizzo's Firearms?"

"You're the son." Buford, with a smile, "And your dad is still, well," fading.

"Yeah."

Buford gave a nod, pointed at the room where the meeting would be. "Before karate it's gymnastics, and before gymnastics it's dance. Have you met Arnie? I was the one who originally sold him the unit. Brilliant idea, really. Never an unused hour." Buford said AA was the first tenant because—although Arnie himself was not a believer in any higher power—he saw a reliable business model. For which Buford could not fault him. Take his own case. Never missed a week. Buford was fifteen years clean today. This was the last place Buford had wandered to for help, he told Nick, with an apologetic note in his voice.

"It was a copper mine that cost me everything," Buford said. "Not that it matters. Before I had the chance to realize how bad I had been fucked I was living on my sister's couch. Didn't take long for her to kick me out. I guess technically I was living on the floor. My back couldn't take the couch. I slept on the tiles in the hallway. The only thing I liked better than blacking out was staying up for a few days straight. Some nights I went on ten-mile runs in my sandals. My sister got tired of it, and who could blame her. I had nothing. I mean nothing. After that I was living in a Walmart parking lot. Not that I cared. All that I cared about was staying high. My sister died. Breast cancer. But that couldn't slow me down. I missed the funeral. I was still too busy smoking crack next to a dumpster at a Circle K. Got arrested outside a Walgreens on Thunderbird for shoplifting. Had my face smashed into the concrete while they were handcuffing me, and it took that whack on the head for me to wake up and realize I needed to change. I spoke about it right here fifteen years ago. I'm the luckiest man alive. I feel lucky for my own life. And I don't mean that in a self-aggrandizing way, I hope it doesn't seem like that. I owe it all to this group. These were the only people who thought I deserved another chance."

Buford might have had more to say, but he stopped to smile at Matt Wilson, who had joined them. Matt offered a fist pound before asking Nick if he could borrow the van.

Matt, whispering: "We're going to take a quick ride."

Nick saw a woman on the phone walking down the sidewalk, then asked: "And if it turns into something longer?" A legitimate question. "How am I supposed to get home?"

"I'd be happy to give you a ride," Buford said. Then, with sudden self-effacement: "Not to pry."

Matt, taking the keys: "The universe hears you."

5

His father, this thin, looked like another man. It showed in his chest and neck—the bones, the hollow skin. His attenuated father. It did not help that his head was shaved.

"Hello." Rizzo tapped the phone against the glass. A sardonic knocking. "Hello?"

"Don't piss off the guards."

"You mean Salvatore," Rizzo said, pointing over his shoulder. "Don't worry about Salvatore. He owes me fifty bucks."

"What do you mean owes you?"

Rizzo slouched and rolled his head. In the brief pause those talking nearby could be heard: faint pleas, promises.

"I can have Salvatore meet you in the parking lot with a Snickers," Rizzo said. "King-sized. I've made a friend whose wife works for Hershey."

"Does that have something to do with why you shaved your head?"

"No. My head is shaved in solidarity with Jeremy, who has cancer."

"You look small. Like sick small."

"It's called getting in shape. I've got a physical trainer, Tristan Delancey. You should see the triceps on this guy. I pay him in fish sticks. I'll have him draft up a regimen for you."

"That's okay."

"So what's the news? You're getting laid?"

"I don't see how that's relevant."

"I'm in jail, Nicholas. It's always relevant. Tell me something good."

"Okay." Silence. "Do you remember Buford Bellum?"

Rizzo, whispering: "What did you just say to me?"

"He's been really impressed with what I'm doing. Like, with the social media for the shop. And I told him my idea about starting my own firm. Consulting small businesses on digital. He loved it. He's going to let me run the social campaigns for businesses in his portfolio. I'm going to help small business owners just like you with their digital marketing."

Rizzo, body coiled: "What did I do that was so bad to you, Nicholas?"

"What do you mean?"

"Tell me. Please. I want to know. What did I ever do besides love you, my son? Oh, what a crime! Poor you with a father who loves him, who makes his son a TV star."

"But Dad, that's not—"

"Television. You know how many people would kill to be on television? I can tell you there are in fact people who kill to be on television, Nick, because I am currently in prison with an insane guy, okay, who killed to be on fucking television! I'm serious. This guy murdered his mom with an ice pick because he thought it would get him his own version of Jerry Springer for the Islamic State. His name is Earl McGurt. He's not even Muslim."

"But Dad, I'm in the shop less now. If I pull off this stuff for Buford? I'll be done with guns. Like you wanted."

Rizzo closed his eyes, put his forehead on the shelf below the glass. "Nick, as my son, I need you to listen to me. Buford Bellum is going to swindle you out of every last cent you've got. You're going to lose my house. You're going to lose it all. Then I'll come out of here with nothing."

Nick, firmly: "Can you please trust me, Dad?"

Long silence.

Rizzo dropped the phone on the cradle.

6

Beneath the unfurling sunup, Nick Rizzo practiced his one good habit:
hiking. He was relieved by the trails. He inhaled the smoky smell of the
kicked-up earth, his calves burning as he reached toward another plane,
panting. There were snake holes, scattered cholla, piles of horse shit, caps
of quartz. The world was brown, green, blue. Sediment clacked down the
mountainside. He stopped on jagged ledges, above the ovular arms of
prickly pears, his hands behind his head, listening to the humbling rasp
of his own breath. Pick a higher power, they said. He picked the dry and
scalding nature of his home.

Sometimes he slipped, he rolled an ankle, he limped and muttered
along, alone. A patch of sweat above his stomach, a faint layer of dust
coated the thighs of his shorts. No matter which trail he took, which
mountain he visited—Thunderbird, Hayden, Camelback—he stared at his
boots while he walked up. Still he came away feeling he had experienced
the terrain. It was a winter-and-spring love. Summers went by hiding in
the central air. On the trail he felt alive. He grew up here in the siltstone.

Today Nick and Matt made their way up A Mountain, an unfortunately named single peak in Tempe with a giant "A" on its southern face.

"I'm so grateful, man," Matt said. He had talked nonstop up the
steepest part of the trail. "That you believe in me? That you trust me with
the shop? Like, this is what I need." Matt struck his palm with the fist
of the other hand. "My dad was a blue-collar guy, man. He worked all
day, all night, because work was what made him feel like he mattered."

"Dude, your dad was an orthopedic surgeon," Nick said. "He retired at, like, fifty."

"All I mean is I want the same sense of pride in who I am, in what I'm doing," Matt said. He stopped to repeat himself with the sun at his back. "I just want to focus on the work. Not the outcomes, but the work. That's where the peace is. Elise told me that, and I can't stop thinking about it."

"Elise," panting. "What happened to Jessica?"

"I'm not, like, with Elise or anything," resuming his easy strides. "I'm not sure she's into me. She's young, man. Like twenty? I met her at the gym. I get this sense that she wants to become a nun. Insane degree of commitment. She eats tuna from the can."

Nick looked around as if expecting to find her here. "Just don't mess this up." He set his elbows on a metal rail. "I don't care if you're fucking a nun, but I need the money from the shop."

"Trust me," Matt said. "I can do it. It's a big responsibility, it's a big challenge, but that's what I need. Things are coming together. I'm around good people, you know? I mean, look at you. You got clean, figured it all out, you've worked your ass off to make this business a success. Elise, she's all about listening, about understanding. She helps people, man. She's got causes, she's got aspirations, she's like really into fitness. Now I've got my chance. I'm grateful, Nick. Thank you. Seriously. Thanks for believing in me, man."

7

He remembered being in a cul-de-sac, stumbling next to a parked car. The many nights ill on the roadside, head hanging out the window of a vehicle, indifferent, unsurprised—he now recalled it all at random. Waiting in a gas station parking lot, the spectacular lights above the pumps. In the back of a stranger's truck. Dozens of candles, everyone nodding off on the couch. Calling, calling again, everyone in the same room waiting. Powder. Burned foil, a lonely spoon. Matches, grill lighters, the stovetop flames. Everyone laughing, stumbling. Punching holes in a bedroom door—the men took turns, for fun. Dinner at dawn. Stealing the cushioned furniture off hotel patios. He lived for the space between days. On a beanbag in his own piss. Facedown on the carpet. Head against the steering wheel. Choking in the hospital bed, plastic attached to his mouth.

Nick feared himself identical to all that he remembered.

8

Matt Wilson

Wednesday 7:13PM

should i turn ac off

has the key ever just like not worked

does the toilet usually make sound

nvm got it lol

actually wait wheres plunger

has toilet ever just gushed water everywhere

whats best way to dry carpet

hey just wanted to confirm code for alarm

what should i do if code doesnt work?

best way to stop alarm besides code???

cops lol

9

HALLELUJAH LANDSCAPING

SPONSORED

Tired of playing phone tag to schedule a landscaper? Welcome to Hallelujah: www.hallelujahlandscaping.com

THE EIFFEL TOWER DEALERSHIP

SPONSORED

Everyone needs a car, but no one needs a salesman. Check out the Eiffel Tower Dealership's salesmen-free online marketplace for your next vehicle: www.eiffeltowercars.com

PHX HOME HOSPICE

SPONSORED

Dying is hard. We make it easy: www.phxhomehospice.com

GARDEN2CLICK2TABLE

SPONSORED

Use code cucumber2 for a 10% discount on your first order! www.gardenclick.com

PRETTY PAWS DOGGY TREATS

SPONSORED

Thanks to our friends at @azrepublic for the great writeup on how we're disrupting the dog treat industry, one pretty paw at a time! www.azrepublic/customizabledoggytreat.com

PHX HOME HOSPICE

SPONSORED

Hospice belongs in the home www.phxhomehospice.com

GARDEN2CLICK2TABLE

SPONSORED

When you need a lime but can't stand the line: www.gardenclick.com

HALLELUJAH LANDSCAPING

SPONSORED

Book your landscaping on a cadence that works for you. Online. Use the code facebookholy to receive 20% off your first yard cleanse: www.hallelujahlandscaping.com

THE EIFFEL TOWER DEALERSHIP

SPONSORED

Ever seen a car lot that reaches into the troposphere? www.eiffeltowercars.com

PHX HOME HOSPICE

SPONSORED

"I wanted him to die with dignity in the same bed where he slept with my mom," says PHX HH customer and son Steven Greenwich @ www.phxhomehospice.com

PRETTY PAWS DOGGY TREATS

SPONSORED

Giving puppies the freedom to bone: www.pretttypawsdogtreats.com

RIZZO DIGITAL

SPONSORED

The marketing arm behind the most popular gun store in Arizona, Rizzo's Firearms, is now helping small to mid-sized businesses across the entire country build and scale their digital marketing. 50% of small businesses fail before the 5 year mark. Don't be 1 of them. Schedule a free consultation today @ www.rizzoconsulting.com

10

What was wrong at the WeWork?

Oh, just the door. It was a faulty-fob situation. Nick looked on as Buford Bellum rammed his shoulder against a door made almost entirely of glass. He shook the handle before ramming the door again.

"Waffle House," Buford said. Now he was making a call on speakerphone and stared up at a security camera. "Last week some kid had a seizure on the ping pong table in here," dragging a hand across his face. "Combination of Red Bull, Vyvanse, and Klonopin." Silence. "Hello? Jeremy? Are you in the elevator?" He stared at the screen.

After the last visit to his father, how was Nick, you know, feeling?

He was feeling fantastic. There were challenges, yes, but Nick understood the necessity of being challenged. Matt Wilson had said it some mornings ago: look at all Nick had accomplished! And all that he still wanted to achieve. To be done with guns. And he would be. He could trust Matt, he had to trust Matt, he had given Matt control over the shop because he knew, with confidence, that there was no reason to worry.

But what about when he found the shop closed?

It was a surprise, yes.

Closed?

It was unfortunate. Closed on a Sunday afternoon. The shop should've been opened hours earlier. Nick stood in front of the tinted windows, peering inside while he listened to Matt's voicemail again.

When he unlocked the front door, he found nothing out of order in the main area of aisles. Back by the displays, all good. Even cleaner than Nick expected. He popped his head into the warehouse, and that was where he found Matt sitting behind the desk. He was not crying in a dramatic fashion. "I just can't do it," Matt said.

11

Elise Allsworth was a southpaw, and she favored her front hook, a tight right swing she clipped to the body and then the head, doubling up before she pumped the straight left. Nick stood with his shoulder behind the heavy bag, rumbling with her punches.

People in headgear bounced around the ring against the far wall; an impressively pregnant woman shadowboxed in front of the wall of mirrors, slipping and uppercutting, while next to her a shirtless man with a vertical scar down his chest swung a sledgehammer against a tire. Stationary fans chopped through the heat. Rap played from ceiling speakers. A bald man with a walker wobbled around saying *jab, jab*. Elise had her hair pulled back tight and a headband covered her forehead. She doubled up her hook once more, almost landed a glove against the face of a speaking Nick, who had an ear against the leather as he asked if she might, you know, consider talking to Matt? "Who?" She hit the bag again.

"Matt," yelling over the pop of the gloves.

"Matt Morales?" She stopped punching, stood back, gave a look like, finally.

"No," pausing. "Wilson."

"Oh." She picked up her water bottle with her wrists. "He's the one, wait, I think I remember," another sip.

"He's having a tough time." Nick, panting, winced a bit as he stretched his chest. "He's in recovery, he's been sober for a while, but I'm worried about him. And I know he's really enjoyed talking to you."

Elise nodded at the clock. "I need to eat in the next thirty minutes." She used her teeth to untie a glove. "Are you hungry?"

Nick met her off Baseline at a McDonald's that was renovated to look like a crashed aerial device: bronze heat-resistant siding, in offset squares. Elise carried a gallon jug of water inside and ordered four double cheeseburgers.

At the table, swinging a protein shaker, she explained that each double cheeseburger had twenty-five grams of protein, but because there was a single slice of cheese, the double cheeseburger was only one dollar, or four times less than the quarter pounder with its two slices. "Cheap easy protein," Elise said. Which she needed: she wanted to fight at one forty-five, but she always had been an undersized kid, and now she was burning several thousand calories a day. Ran miles before sunup. Sparred in the afternoons. Knocked out a lift before bed. The degree of difficulty changed—she had a propensity to overwork: once pushing the declension of a calf raise so far that she partially tore her Achilles—but the routine remained consistent, nothing missed or skipped.

She unwrapped each burger in the same calculated way, Nick noticed. Top fold, side folds, last fold—all before she lifted for a bite.

Elise was a kid. Matt had been right to call her young. Early twenties, tops. She had on a shirt over her sports bra. Light patches of acne showed on her face, above and below each of her blue eyes. Veins cut down her forearms. Nick glanced over his own arms, which seemed disproportionately small given the unfortunate size of his digestive area. Could Nick box, too? Was that what was missing from his life? A routine beating. The idea of being punched was enough to jolt his heart.

So, boxing? He wanted to know why she did it. If he understood, was the thought, then maybe, for himself?

"I don't know." She was done eating, all the burger wrappers neatly stacked on the tray. "Do you remember that shooting? The one, at the high school, when no one died?"

Nick, leaning forward. "Excuse me?"

"The Mass Survival, or whatever. Just because no one literally died, as in got shot and bled out, doesn't mean there wasn't, like, a spiritual death. A whole generation of kids basically had their spirits murdered that day. In my opinion. I mean. And I was one of them."

"Totally," Nick said. He was looking around at the tables, trying to think up an excuse to run out the door. "So you were there? Like in the school?"

"Front and center," Elise said.

In fact, she was dead, she felt, for hours after the shooting stopped. Let her explain. She was in first period when it happened. Her language arts class. Mr. Calhoun, in the corner, behind his laptop, playing YouTube videos related to their assigned reading—Hemingway. A packed room, barely enough desks for the forty or so bodies, barely enough space for the forty or so desks. The chairs of the rearmost desks rested against the closets. There came sounds like smashed bricks. Everyone seemed to understand, yet no one moved. More shots. Mr. Calhoun closed his laptop, but the overhead projector remained on, a blue square across the wall. Someone turned off the lights, locked the door. They had practiced this many times, the lockdown drills, rehearsed for at least a decade—it was the true constant of their education—and the class sank methodically toward the rear corner of the room, a procedural sadness in their steps, carefully overturning desks, whimpering, curling on the carpet. They folded into one another, the students, pressing themselves into a single mass. But one stayed at his desk as if images continued to play across the wall. Terrified into stasis. Tim Ortiz. No matter the whispered encouragements or pleas or threats telling him to leave his desk and hide, Tim acted as if he did not hear a single thing—he sat looking straight ahead—like he had stopped time, departed his body, drifted into the space between the projector and the screen. Elise was on her back in the corner of the room. She could recount what she had heard then, what she was told. The door to their room was supposed to be locked but the shooter walked in. She knew him as a name, understood they shared hallways, an assembly room, a nurse's office, nothing more.

For her the experience was all sound. The ceiling pitched in dark waves as she listened to the bullets. Every surface fogged with pain. There was heat. The air was thick. Screams. She knew they were hit and holed and agape, dying. But then, without warning: orders. A cop, in the room, yelling, pulled Tim from the desk. None of it was real, Elise said. She was convinced she had died in the silence preceding the shots, that she was still dead as she marched with the other students through the halls outside into the screeching daylight, the last departure. She was leaving, she had left. It was the purest feeling, she said. No pressure, no fear. It was over. It was finally over. All that could be had been. Her classmates formed a line in the parking lot, weeping against the fence. Elise moved through familiar spaces with a new detachment, certain she was waiting for the next phase, until much later that night when she took out her contacts. It sounded strange, she knew. She pinched the plastic from her eyes before sleep. But she was surprised to find her vision still poor, her own image in the bathroom a speckled blur. It was this failure of sight that convinced her she was among the living.

The rows of tables, Nick noticed, emanated the same disturbing shine.

"I'm not a victim," Elise was saying. "I don't need, like, pity. And to me it's not even a debate. To me it's all about common sense. It's obvious people should not own guns."

"I couldn't agree more," Nick said. His thigh jumped beneath the table, he tore at the fingernail of his left thumb.

"But I forgive that kid. I forgive everyone. What happened was horrible," she said, "but I've moved on with my life. And yeah, it was tough, at first."

Several of her classmates went on to Harvard, Yale, Princeton, Columbia, each one promising to be the next corporate revolutionary, social media change agent. Others slithered into the corners of their families, no interest in college, in career ladders, showing up for their graveyard shifts and then keeping the blinds drawn in their bedrooms all day, microwaving meals. Tim Ortiz—the kid who couldn't leave his desk—joined that growing legion sucked dry from drugs. And Elise? Well, she considered herself a member of the most common group. That is, ambivalent.

She wanted to do good. She said this with a tone of slight exhaustion. She was well aware, she said, of all those who *wanted* to do good, who *purported* to do good, but who ultimately achieved nothing. The volunteering she did was fine, but it was also predictable, clichéd. She wanted something bigger, something for all the mass shooting survivors in America, a way to help transition back into living. Not that she was the expert, she said. She was living with her parents, fully dependent, but she got into boxing, she got into volunteering, distracted herself enough to function in some basic sense. Deleted all her social media. Made an effort to stay offline. She was the only person she knew with a flip phone. Teaching boxing to mass shooting survivors? She loved boxing for the simplicity. She knew it sounded crazy, but the only thing she could compare it to was prayer.

"I grew up going to church, but it was just a thing that I did," Elise said. "It wasn't until I started boxing that I really felt attached to church. Not to Jesus or anything. I'm not really into Jesus. But I like church, I like the consistency of it. You know? Raise your hands, lower your hands, bow your head, palms together. And that matters? That's amazing. So I've become like a total OCD person, I know it's weird," pointing toward her folded burger wrappers. "But routine makes me feel so calm."

12

It could be morally permissible to withhold the truth. Yes, sometimes you had to lie. For example: he told no one what he saw when he died. Even his father—no, especially his father. How could he? More questions than answers. To say it was to condemn himself to a world he no longer understood.

He was a child, searching through bushes at the side of an unsettling brick house. It was a neighborhood of rich lawns. The shadows, the shadows were immense, the shadows came from nothing and cut across the lawns. There was total silence but he never felt afraid.

Lively row of bushes, green with little red dots, slender branches. What was Nick looking for? No way to recall but he knew it felt urgent, worth the effort. He kneeled in the grass, hands in the bushes, struck in the face by the leaves.

A whistle from an old train. It came from a hill of grass, a hill higher than the surrounding houses, and at the peak of the hill was a man in shadow who he knew to be his father: Rizzo, with a pleasant swing to his arms. His father smiled, so happy. And then Rizzo stood over him. His father said nothing, just stood and stared.

Rizzo reached out, lowered a hand toward his son, grabbed the back of his neck in a way that was almost tender. At first. It all began as this tender thing, Rizzo holding his neck, pulling him close, lifting him off his knees. But then he kept pulling, kept lifting. Soon he was either hugging Nick with so much love, or he was killing Nick, strangling him, but he was so clumsy that it looked like love.

Everything around Nick became a question. Whose house was this? This yard, these bushes? And this neighborhood, why was no one else outside on a day with this much sun? No cars either, why? The clouds? He did not know. He realized he never knew. And then he was alive. It was no different than a dream. And like a dream, it meant there was reason to believe in something beyond, in the existence of mysteries. What else could it mean?

Nick needed several matches to light his cigarette. He was on the patio, on a chair, here in real life, smoking, in the purple evening. He folded the pack in half, bent a match head between the paper, swiped his fingers. There was a pop, a sizzle. He was at a stone table, in a metal chair, struck by the heat.

But the guilt was relentless. The guilt reduced time to a pathetic murmur in his chest. When his eyes were open he wanted them closed, but as soon as his eyes closed he needed them open. He was on his bed, unable to breathe, waiting for the ceiling to fall. He stood in front of the microwave. Opened the fridge, found only the shelves. Into bed again. Then up to pull the blinds. Then up to find the remote. In the kitchen again, but now with the remote in his hand. The sagging elm beside a driveway, its branches burdened by ropy leaves.

He knew Elise would find out. He would apologize, he would request the right to explain. She would be gone. He knew it. She would be gone. There was no point in tracing the thought to its sinking conclusion. He knew what would happen. He did not deserve a friend whom he had already hurt so terrifically.

But it was also his own, his past. His to tell? He did not want to be the person he was yesterday. He wanted to will himself new through a lean retelling.

13

A bowl of holy water. It was nested in the wall of the church's atrium. The process should have been simple. Dip, dab, be on your way. Plenty of those who stepped past Nick did just that, tapping the surface with a finger and commencing the cross, but Nick was tentative—not wanting to overdo—which meant his finger was mostly dry when it blessed his head.

He was supposed to wait here for Elise and Matt, in the hexagonal room, but his gift for being in the way made this difficult: through the crowd he shuffled, smiled, apologized, turned left, turned right, tripped over children. Families, on their way into mass, smiling. Nick felt sure that they were smiling at his unfortunately conspicuous reality. He made his way back to the bowl, stuck a finger in, surprised at the cool depth of the water.

"What happened to your face?" It was Matt, who smelled of smoke.

Nick, touching his forehead: "Did you tell Elise that you worked at a gun shop?"

"Of course not. Dude, she hates guns," Matt said. He stuck half a hand in the water and then rubbed at a stain on his shirt.

"That's holy water," Nick said.

"So it doesn't work on chocolate?"

Elise peeled off the end of the latest arrivals and smacked Matt on the shoulder with the parish's newsletter. "Asshole," she whispered, with a smile.

The visiting priest to Saint Joseph's was Father Bill. This was a problem only for Nick Rizzo. There he was, right in the middle of a center pew, covering his eyes with a hand after he looked over his shoulder to find the Father himself—devout supporter of Rizzo's Firearms—traveling down the aisle as the music boomed. Nick considered kneeling for the entire mass, disguising himself as a committed penitent. It was a modest church with no easy exits.

After mass Father Bill was outside shaking hands, receiving praise. Framed by the doors, he seemed to have stepped down from the light. "Ah, Nick," Father Bill said. "It's been too long. How are things?"

Nick stood with his teeth clenched and said things were absolutely splendid—he tried to pull away before Elise might hear more, but Father Bill held on for an extra beat.

"And your father," Father Bill said.

Well, you know. Rizzo was still, uh, his father.

"We pray," Father Bill said.

They were on their way to the car when Elise asked how he knew Father Bill. "We have mutual friends," Nick said.

Elise was in a summer dress, it started below her shoulders and ended above the knees and her arms showed the three-part division of the seasoned lifter. "And your dad," she said. She brought the sun visor down, touched up her mascara. "He's okay?"

She asked the question with such sincerity that Nick considered pretending to suffer a seizure to spare her the lie. "He's as good as he can be," he said.

"Sick?"

"Very," swatting the blinker as he waited to make a left. He glanced in the rearview at Matt, who had his sunglasses on and his head toward the window. "A very sick man."

"I'd be happy to visit with you. I go to hospice all the time with my friend Felicia," Elise said.

"That's really not necessary," with more irritation than he intended. Softer: "He wouldn't want you to see him like this. Hey—Matt? How are we doing?"

"My stomach," Matt said. He hunched over in the seat. "Is raw as fuck."

"Okay." Lower, back to Elise: "I was thinking about what you said the other day. Like, about helping?"

14

ATTENTION: Only 29 Days Left!
Mass Survival Foundation nick@masssurvivalfoundation.org
via auth.cclist.com
to me

Dear Fellow Life Advocate,

There Are Only 29 Days Left
To Hit Our $10K Goal
Consider Gifting Life Today

The Mass Survival Foundation seeks to be the first organization
of its kind: a **nonprofit dedicated to helping survivors of mass
shootings** transition back into the crowded world. By giving **even
$1** today, you'll be contributing to the formation of a counseling
collective to support Mass Shooting Survivors.

AGAINST MASS SHOOTINGS? **GIVE TODAY**

15

PHX HOME HOSPICE @phxhh · July 18
summer smells: phxhh aids with daily fresh flowers brought to your dying loved one's bedside #tulips #littlethings #grieving

PHX HOME HOSPICE @phxhh · July 18
let us make your last wishes come true #happy #death

PHX HOME HOSPICE
SPONSORED
Avondale economics teacher & PHX HH customer Kevin puts it best: "Don't let death be difficult."
www.phxhomehospice/kevinbestietestimonial.com

PHX HOME HOSPICE @phxhh · July 18
never die alone again #unity

PHX HOME HOSPICE @phxhh · July 18
newest @cdcgov health system review reports record malpractice claims: bit.ly/97bosoX #healthsystems #wtf

ATTENTION: Only 28 Days Left To Stop Mass Shootings!
Mass Survival Foundation nick@masssurvivalfoundation.org
via auth.cclist.com
to me

Dear Fellow Human,

Who Believes In Our Right To Co-Exist
In Crowds Without Fear Of Being Shot
There Are Only 28 Days Left
To Hit Our $10K Goal
Which Will Help Fight The Wealthy
Pro-Mass-Shooting Organizations

The Mass Survival Foundation seeks to be the first organization
of its kind: a **nonprofit dedicated to helping survivors of mass
shootings** by combating pro-gun organizations. By giving **even $5**
today, you'll help fund the efforts against mass shootings.

Do You Believe In Life? **GIVE TODAY**

PHX HOME HOSPICE

SPONSORED

Death is inevitable. Where you die is not. Schedule a free consult
www.phxhomehospice/consult.com

PHX HOME HOSPICE @phxhh · July 19

that feeling when you realize your loved one will be happy at the end
#priceless #gratitude #goneforever

PHX HOME HOSPICE

SPONSORED

Be there from afar. PHX HH offers live cam streaming so that you can
be in the room for your mother's last breath no matter where you live:
www.phxhomehospice/pressrelease/skypartnership.com

PHX HOME HOSPICE @phxhh · July 19

what's as permanent as death? diamonds. that's why we're excited to
announce a 10% discount on all @londongold inventory for PHX HH
customers

PHX HOME HOSPICE @phxhh · July 19

them:
me: where you die should be your decision!

PHX HOME HOSPICE @phxhh · July 20

proud to be supported by @divinecross & @tacobell #partnerships #lastrites #nachochalupa #morefiresauceplease #viaticum

PHX HOME HOSPICE @phxhh · July 20

louder for the people in the back: #deathbelongsinthehome

18

ATTENTION: Only 27 Days Left To Be Against Mass Shootings!
Mass Survival Foundation nick@masssurvivalfoundation.org
<u>via</u> auth.cclist.com
to me

How Are You Supporting Survivors?

The Mass Survival Foundation seeks to be the first organization
of its kind: a **nonprofit dedicated to helping survivors of mass
shootings** by providing **comprehensive resources** for their road to
recovery. By giving **even $10** today, you'll be able to help others.

Not A Mass Shooter? **GIVE TODAY**

19

Here was what the video would have shown, had it been posted.

A man on a knee in the desert. The sky the color of rust. There's breathing, audible, from the person recording. The kneeling man has a green tube across his shoulder. It's historic, obsolete, a rocket launcher from a decade of tremendous prosperity. Is it that heavy? The man, posing, wobbles in his stance, showing the uncertainty of inexperience. Chatter increases off screen. Shouts, undecipherable. He's pretending to take aim at something over the horizon. He tightens his stance, making himself smaller, squeezing his arm around the tube. Which is when it happens: a whooshing flame. The explosion happens at his back, he slides across the gravel facedown. Cheers, laughter. The camera wobbles to track the rocket.

Here the shouts lose their energy. The camera trembles, there's movement. A boom. A flash of light. Smoke rises from a strip mall unit. Then the flames, which never end.

20

What was dying like?

It crashed all at once, cooling the organs. The point at which he ceased to be: an answer—satisfying, immediate—to the problem known as his life. When had he been any good at living? Or so Nick was reminded.

Was anyone hurt in the explosion?

Unfortunately not.

But it was an accident?

"I'm so fucking sorry, man." Matt, on the phone, his voice shaking. He said he had been trying to come up with some sick promotional content, the rocket launcher from Danny was the only prop. "I'm sorry, Nick. I really am. Just tell me what to do. I'm sorry. Please. I don't want to go to jail. I'm so sorry, man. Just tell me what to do."

So?

Nick got to the building not long after the firefighters, granting him a few minutes to witness the demise. He parked in the middle of the street, watching. The entrance to the business park's cul-de-sac was blocked off. Fire trucks, flashing lights. Employees from the neighboring businesses in the strip mall had been evacuated and now stood on the sidewalk holding up their phones. Only smoke remained, black bunches rolling off the foam roof. Cracks, pops. The firefighters were already packing up to leave, a few carrying heat-warped material. The consensus was that, with all the ammunition inside, it was a miracle everyone survived.

21

Buford Bellum pulled into the driveway with the right side of his Cadillac's hood crushed toward the windshield. "There was a misunderstanding," Buford said, after Nick pointed at the car. Buford wore a stained tuxedo blazer. He had acquired a limp.

They stood with their backs to the garage. Other than their voices the neighborhood was silent. It was the purple sky of midnight, hot even for August.

Nick was being pushed out of the real estate for Rizzo's Firearms. Or not just pushed out, but threatened with financial ruin. Legal fees. More lawsuits expected, dozens likely. Hearing loss was the most common. The Property Owners Association had filed an excess of grievances. It was no surprise that the UK conglomerate—to whom Buford had sold everything around Rizzo's shop—wanted a frozen yogurt store in its place, and their offer to buy the strip mall unit from Nick was humiliatingly low even given the cost to remodel after the fire. It was more than the explosion, the POA cases said. It was also the people Matt left unsupervised at the shop, some of whom evidently were practicing "lewd" and "bewildering" behaviors in front of, inside of, and most frequently behind the shop, leading to complaints. Quorum was met, votes were cast.

"Financially what are your options?" Buford asked this while staring straight ahead. "You have to first evaluate your options."

"I'm selling the house," Nick said. "It's one of those things. Short-term loss, long-term gain. So I'll sell, wait out some of the legal stuff, and if I scale my own business? And I will scale. You know I'll scale. Look at the metrics for the home hospice marketing. The conversion rates are insane. So I'll buy a house twice as big in less than a year."

"One idea," Buford said, before he recommended Nick sell him the house. "You could always buy it back," he added.

22

Don't worry: Nick had everything under control.

He did?

He was making adjustments, but he was also busy. There was so much to do.

For example?

Oh, it was almost too much to list.

Oh?

It was, actually, too much to list.

But if pressed for an incomplete list?

The more familiar a process, the more unknown its inner workings.

Okay, but even one example?

Deciding on a movie to watch. For example.

Thanks for clarifying, but—

And then there was *Jackass*. Not full episodes, though. He came across clips. So much began to make sense. There were clips of men volunteering to be electrocuted, being gnawed by small alligators, shot with rubber bullets, punched by prizefighters, clamped by rat traps. To watch was to study slices of himself. All the school-day afternoons! How could he have forgotten the ass of a man in a thong, an ass tattooed with YOUR NAME, and the two cheeks being pierced, joined with a metal bar? How could he have forgotten two shirtless friends slapping each other across their chests, taking turns, laughing, screaming, go? A used toilet plunger smashed into a face? Two men in a shopping cart flying down an alley in hopeful fraternity, swerving into a brick wall?

Well—

And as if he was not busy enough, he watched videos of fights, compilations of sanctioned knockouts. He never fought—he had surprised himself more than his father that day, he thought, when he turned from the door of the Eldorado to swat his father in the face—but now he could not stop watching videos of mixed martial arts. He liked the name of the sport, its confounding reach, able to encompass almost any manner of combat as its referent. He liked that as soon as the fighter won he was hurriedly wrapped in brands. Hats, shirts, flags. He liked the replays, the slow shake of flesh on the face as consciousness shut off like a whip of city steam. He liked the shift in angles, the overhead shot of the octagonal cage, and the padded floor printed with logos: Modelo—the beer brand displayed across the padded floor, with dried blood across its name.

Was there anything he would not watch?

Nothing that he had come across. Undeterred, he was, by video of all forms of disaster: hurricanes, tornadoes, tsunamis, city floods, forest fires, genocides, police murders, drone strikes, freeway pileups, derailed trains, old war footage, new war footage, 9/11, suicide bombers, plane crashes, beheadings, mass shooters.

How did it all come to be?

From cell phones, from body cams, from drones, from Go-Pros. The clumsier the recording, the more authentic it could be said to be.

Was death the paragon of authenticity?

It was impossible to falsify.

These videos—were they only about entertainment? Or also edification?

Neither: he watched to seal off the disquiet that lurked in stillness. He never shed the nervousness that came from being truly alone.

Soon he sought out ads from his childhood, the early-morning infomercials he had watched when he had been too nervous to sleep. The Total Gym. Chuck Norris and Christie Brinkley, confidently reserved, assuredly fit, demonstrating to real people on the boardwalk the *new self* one could achieve with their product. He liked the focus on function, with the goal of encouraging you to pick up the phone and call now. The early mornings in bed watching this exact infomercial on his Zenith, and the last thing he saw before sleep was a full rotation of this exercise machine, which he now thought looked medieval. It was different with OxiClean. The infomercial he remembered well—the bullish pitchman, Billy Mays, in his khakis, with his stainless-steel watch, pointing hard at the camera—but it was different knowing that Billy Mays had died. Nick watched. He rewatched. How could a video continue if the person no longer did? Was Billy Mays less alive now than the product? Neither living nor dead: inanimate?

Was he losing his mind? Or was the world? This thought alone induced an unbearable degree of agita.

What else gave Nick agita?

The blank screen, the buffer circle sign, the slow load; video with no audio, stalled video with accurate audio; the flashing battery icon, cracks in his screen; vibrations from an incoming call, from a received text; when he stared at his screen deciding whether to answer, and when he deleted again a response he had typed, and when he clicked through his messages and realized he had forgotten to ever respond; being the only person in the room not on his phone; scrolling without a plan to watch; the vibration from a voicemail; his own reflection in the screen in his hand; how the size of the screen compared to his hand; when he could not find his phone; when he found his phone, and learned he had no new calls, no new texts; when a feared voicemail became a robot message; strangers with ringtones; those who took a call in a crowd as if they were alone, and those in a crowd who continued to ignore their ringing phones.

At around midnight Nick read all the comments on the Rizzo's Firearms ad. More than two thousand, not including the comments on the comments. Most, alarmingly supportive. He believed the comments more than he did his own thoughts. There was an authority to these, a democratic coherence that his own thoughts were without. The ad had been viewed more than eight hundred thousand times. He tried to remember the exact numbers, the views, the comments, so he could witness them increase, so he might grow with them. Or he did, at first. How did he seem to those he would never know? He could not help but care what they thought for that very reason: because it was impossible to know.

But did he sell the house?

23

"They stopped letting us watch the news again. What's the name of that guy? The Black guy they shot a bunch of times while he was sitting in his car?"

"You mean—"

"And his wife filmed it? Like I said, I haven't seen it, but you hear things."

They sat on opposite sides of the glass. Father, son. Rizzo looked like a figure vanishing through the present. Nick held the landline, waiting. He pushed his hand through his hair, hoped he arranged his face in a way that did not seem too nervous, too terrified. Naturally this was how he felt: nervous, terrified. It was a feeling located unmistakably in the center of his body, breath-affecting. There were men on either side of Rizzo, guards against the far wall, the unsparing light from the ceiling.

"You okay?" It was a question so unexpected and sincere that Nick had the urge to cry. "I mean, you know, sober-wise," Rizzo said.

"I'm more than okay," Nick said. What else could he say? He wanted to sound alive. "I've got some very exciting news," he said. Then he told his father why he sold the house to Buford Bellum.

"Are you trying to fucking kill me? I asked for three things, Nick," holding up the corresponding fingers. "Three simple things. Take care of yourself, take care of the house, and sell the goddamn business. Is that so hard?"

At which point Nick said he had, in fact, done all three: he was clean, the business was, well, gone, and while it might seem like he had fucked up on the house front, he was actually making sure that next year Rizzo came out to something far better, a life worth double the previous square footage. "I know how it seems," Nick concluded.

"I have a question for you," Rizzo said. "And this is not rhetorical. The question is: Have you learned nothing?"

But Nick was already standing. Where was he going? "I guess I'll see you later," Nick said. By later he meant never again. Heard enough, thanks. What did his father know? He was the one in jail!

24

The design of the Dune Mirage came from the one-night motels of a half-century ago. Two floors organized around a green pool. There was a gate, a box you drove up to and entered a code. All the parking spots were covered by metal awnings. Minivans. Old SUVs. Trucks with metal boxes in their beds, a neglected convertible. It was late afternoon, the sun would never set. A bushy-tailed fox trotted through the sunlight, a man stood grilling behind his truck. Exposed stairways. It was easy to imagine the maroon doors all opening on the same scene. This was the apartment complex where Nick Rizzo now lived.

His apartment was a gray one-bedroom, bare, shoddy, with a mass of tangled cables next to an unhung flat-screen. Shelves lined with calaveras, the skulls painted with flowers. Stacked boxes acted as furniture. Matt had insisted on helping with the move—"After all you've done for me, man?"—which first involved transporting furniture from the house into storage, which required more people than Matt and Nick, so Matt's crew—the crew formerly accused of debauchery around Rizzo's Firearms—volunteered to lug articles into storage and through the new apartment's inconveniently angled doorway. They were men in various stages of dishevelment: Matt and his friends, sweating and shouting and exhaustingly unorganized. Nick had tried and failed to be helpful, standing precisely where things needed to land, calling out left when he meant right.

A group of ten or so people moved around the apartment tonight, laughing, hanging out. Some were familiar. There was Brent Stanley, a meeting frequent. Brent was a Newport Beach native who became addicted to crystal meth, a drug that he briefly thought would help his amateur career in powerlifting, until he had a stroke at thirty. Now he was an aspiring bodybuilder hooked on his higher power. He walked around with his shirt off, bouncing his pecs with outward irony. There was Ginny from Boston, a longtime bartender. She sat on the carpet, next to a candle, everyone talking above her. Then there was the man with the letter X tattooed on each eyelid. "Kenny," he said, to Nick, after a fist bump. He was from Pueblo, Colorado, dreamed of being a restaurateur, had come to Arizona for rehab, then found himself in jail. Now eight months sober, he worked as a line cook at a Japanese restaurant. "Hey, I acted in a commercial when I was a kid," he told Nick. "Discount Tire. A tire flies through the air and smashes a window. Then it cuts to all the kids screaming. You remember it? I was one of the screaming kids. My parents wanted me to be an actor, and I thought about it. Ended up dabbling in pornography. Nothing crazy. Regular suck and fuck. But I lost the will. Started to wonder: What do you fuck your heart out for? You fuck so hard, you fuck until you think you're going to die, until you literally can't breathe and feel like your dick will explode, and for what? For an embroidered robe?"

Electronic music played. It was Matt's idea to celebrate the new place with a party, because evidently he felt burning down the gun shop was not enough. A housewarming event, he called it. So here Nick Rizzo was—not so much the man of the hour as the person with a residence; not the life of the party but rather the man who had no choice but to attend; never the entertainer, instead the incompetent host, doubting any word he might offer even to a simple question about the weather—he now wandered through the floating conversations in his apartment, looking for somewhere to stand.

"Eight different angles of impact," said a man in a White Sox hat.

He held up his phone, there was a video on Instagram of a man with a ponytail shooting watermelons with a sniper rifle. @gallaghershoots, the handle. Slow-mo'd videos of exploding fruit. He was a former Navy SEAL who lived alone on Texas land. Unsurprisingly, millions of followers. "The thing about fentanyl is," someone said. A man in a Suns jersey told a woman he had been punched in the face on average once per year. Then, near the lamp, a woman with purple bangs: "Good for you. Seriously. What I always say is do what makes you happy, or whatever. And that's why I think, like, if someone chooses not to be sober, if someone prefers to get high, then that's okay too." A woman in a beanie said: "*Intervention*? How do we expect people to 'recover' after it's revealed that everyone they love has been engaged in a lie on TV? Maybe it's the families who agree to go on *Intervention* who have a disease."

Nick went outside to smoke a pack of cigarettes.

There were three men in hats and earrings, their elbows on the railing, staring down at the pool.

"Tuskegee," one guy said. "Everyone wants to talk about Russia. My response is the same: Tuskegee. Because if the government will give all these Black people syphilis for years and lie about it, what makes you think they wouldn't try to make up some story about Russia to take the election from Trump?"

25

Sumacs almost horizontal. Branches torn, bark drenched. Same with the palms. It was a short but ecstatic downpour. From the sky it seemed a cloud had collapsed into the valley, a black column drilling through the desert floor. The golf course drowned into a bog. Mud water streamed through a culvert. Planes were grounded, trapped on the tarmac. Pools overflowed, spilling little rocks across patios. Saguaros lost their oldest limbs. On the edge of a corral, white horses cried while the water shot across their stables' sheet metal roofs. A group of landscapers—all in long sleeves, bandanas around their necks—stood beneath an eave of a business park, smoking. It was a warm and pummeling rain, the kind felt on the skin long after it dried. It was nearing the end of monsoon season.

Between a pair of crooked trees, on a plot of tended dirt: a bunkerish home with brick archways before the receded entrance, an unconnected carport where a truck was parked facing the street. Someone emerged from the house, walked without rush into the rain. Soon the truck had its headlights on, wipers on, engine humming.

Felicia Ryan was behind the wheel. Her hair was down but she was tying it back, steering with her knee, cigarette between her lips ready to be ashed. The rain pummeled the window. She edged along, truck tires sending waves onto the sidewalks.

She had causes that rotated with the nights: sitting at the IRC welcome desk, and bearing paltry bouquets to home hospice visits, serving spoonfuls of pinto beans onto trays at the shelter. More days than not she felt she made no difference. She had a man named Earl who was an idiot but also a very good fuck. She was happy with her life, more or less. Sometimes the wind hit her and she felt certain she would sob. But more frequent were the days when she walked around smiling, confident she would never die.

The rain ended as Felicia drove down Central. Those she was in search of would soon emerge from under the roofs of strip malls, wandering for copper scrap. Central was almost carless, bordered by an automotive repair shop, a Dollar General, unsponsored billboards. Sections of the street carved by the light rail tracks. A Baptist church that resembled an office building. Off the side streets all the low houses had steel security doors. Miles ahead, past the taller buildings, the sunlight vertically striped the horizon.

Felicia slowed beside a man with a cane, a woman next to him pushed a shopping cart covered with a blue tarp beneath which were unidentifiable electronics. They were dripping water. Felicia rolled her window down, struck by the smell of the wet concrete. She called out in English, then Spanish, then English again. She felt ridiculous. The couple stopped walking, looking toward her car. Felicia got out, grabbed bags of food from the back seat: each bag was filled with a sandwich, an apple, a Gatorade, a card for Saint Vincent de Paul, a five-dollar bill. The pair tucked the bags beneath a strip of tarp, resuming their journey in silence.

Van Buren and Thirty-second Street. She pulled into a Circle K and found along the side of the building near the ice chest the regular crew with a few subtractions. The pattern was very young girls and much older men. Girls around fourteen with men around Felicia's age. Some Felicia had driven to rehab herself—women the size of children with huge purses and bruises under their sunglasses—then inevitably found back here, whittled and scabbed. Today she saw a man nodding off while still standing: he was bent at the waist and his fingers just touched the sidewalk.

"You look not great," she said to Stacey, one of the girls from north Phoenix. She was nineteen, wore a sweatshirt even in the summer. "Where's Vanessa?" She squinted at those against the wall.

"Which Vanessa?" She took a box of needles from Felicia, a few bags of food.

Felecia couldn't remember. She watched Stacey take a seat between a swollen hairless guy and another shaded by a straw fedora.

It was while driving north on Thirty-second Street today that Felicia had unknowingly passed Nick Rizzo, who was speeding in the exact opposite direction. Both their windshields were hit with rainwater splashed by the other's tires. Nick was on his way to the health center that was attached to the steaming prison complex off Roosevelt. As he sped through a shifting stoplight, he looked over at Matt Wilson, his friend in the passenger seat whose face was now the same color as the passing asphalt. Matt wore a long-sleeved shirt and athletic shorts and could not open his eyes. He had been in Nick's bathroom, passed out, barely breathing.

Elise leaned into the front of the car, rummaging in her purse. "Guarantee Felicia has some Narcan," she said. "And she might even be volunteering for hospice right now."

Valleywise Health. Nick left the key in the ignition. Smoke had gathered around the Eldorado's tires. Beneath the yellow windows of the building, Nick and Elise each had an arm of Matt's around their respective necks, carrying their friend toward a trio of hospital workers standing in a circle of cigarettes and phone screens. Nick shouted for help. One guy looked up from his phone and yelled back: "We're waiting for Domino's." The automatic doors of the hospital opened and then closed although nobody was nearby.

They were waiting in line. It was a white and warm and obliterating room. The chairs were bolted to the floor, there were people across the plastic seats. A sheet of glass separated the hospital workers from everyone else. It seemed right to respectfully wait, Nick thought, considering there were several groups enduring the same situation and yet all displayed an experienced patience. Nick, struggling, hooked his arms under Matt's shoulders to keep his sinking friend upright. Elise called out: she kneeled next to her purse, holding up a bottle of Narcan.

Matt, on his back, arms limp. He seemed to be suspended at the end of time. His face was rigid. He was losing all quality of expression. It was here that Elise's hand appeared below his face: her hand, with veined knuckles, powerful grace. She sprayed each nostril with the chemical. Her hand nearing his face, retreating, nearing again. Then gone. The face, just the face. There followed no rapid uprightness, no scream. Not much change at all, really, except to the pacing of the breath, a subtle twitch in the skin. There existed, in all things, a desire to continue. This was what Nick concluded as he studied these movements. He felt something loosen behind his own face.

When he looked up from his friend he saw Felicia at the malfunctioning entrance, staring back at him with an expression of mild annoyance.

26

CONGRATULATIONS: The Fight Never Ends!
Mass Survival Foundation nick@masssurvivalfoundation.org
via auth.cclist.com
to me

Shooters vs. Givers

The Mass Survival Foundation wants to personally thank you. Not in our most optimistic moments could we have expected to raise over $25,000 in our first week. To have brought the 30-day total to over $100,000 is a testament to your amazing generosity.

Now, while we're proud of the success we've had, we also need to remain realistic.

We hate to ask people to give more, so we won't. Instead we say thanks for your kindness, and if you so choose to contribute more to what some say is the greatest existential threat to our species, then you'll receive a free DON'T SHOOT (GIVE!) bumper sticker by using the code generous1.

BE A HUMAN, GIVE TODAY

27

PHX HOME HOSPICE @phxhh · September 6

we all deserve the death of our dreams

28

What was Nick's excuse for the poor funnel metrics?

"Organic isn't doable anymore," Nick said. His elbows were on the table, his hands open beside his face. "It's all about paid marketing," he said. "Which is all about the algorithms. Which are always changing. I forecasted based on methods that are completely irrelevant now. We're basically lighting money on fire. That's why I'm just sticking with stuff for home hospice. Which makes sense. Arizona is where people come to die. At some point we should also look into Nevada. It's really our only hope unless I keep touching the nonprofit money."

He was with Buford Bellum in the eighteenth-floor office of the shared workspace. They were moving out, though they both seemed to be waiting for the other to begin lifting things. The room had enough space for a desk, two plastic chairs, the few stacked boxes. The windows behind Buford looked out on the unfilled condos above the receded town lake.

"That's fine to tell me," Buford said, scrolling. He was dressed casually. "But the investors are going to have questions for you. Lots of questions. Are you prepared for that? I won't be able to help."

"What do you mean?"

"The meeting is during the annual Taco Bell's Franchisee Conference in Albuquerque. It's a time of learning, bonding, networking, and reviewing the risk of potential *E. coli*," Buford said, locking his phone, "Try to remember that we all take losses. That's essential to being an entrepreneur. Losing. Now, sometimes those losses add up. Sometimes those losses feel insurmountable. But have faith in logic, Nick. Because the universe is logical. It might take some time, you might need to weather the storm for longer than you would like, but in the end it will all work out."

But Nick could call Elise, right?

She refused to talk. On the phone, over text, email. No response. Even about nonprofit stuff. Felicia had told her. Nick Rizzo? Don't you know? And that was the end.

But overall was he, well, still, you know, sober?

He was fine. Sober. Whatever.

Fine?

He often caught himself staring at a search bar without knowing what to type.

He was staying in bed past noon. He listened to the click of the ceiling fan. And food, well, seemed less essential. He ate standing from bags and tubs and rectangular containers. No plates, no bowls. A spoon would do. There were loaves of bread in the freezer from before his father went to prison. He stood with the freezer door open, certain he would be outlived by the grains. Watching *Wheel of Fortune*, he got up only to piss during a brief commercial break. Was it time for a haircut? But how should his hair be cut? To a barber, to a hairdresser, he could not remember what he had ever said. The morning hikes? Too far. The drive, he meant. Instead the hours before sunrise were spent on his phone, in bed. Today Nick came across the profile for Brian Sands, a high school friend who had run around with fake diamond studs in his ears and a shaved head. Nick had not heard from him in years, more than a decade now, yet he knew from Facebook that Brian was in a prison outside Prescott for another botched robbery, with a tattoo on his chest that reached to the base of his throat. Nick found a picture from two years earlier that Brian had posted: pair of white Jordans, printer, vacuum cleaner, music stand, baseball hats, hit me up in the comments for the price. The few comments were from people Nick did not recognize but who seemed to know Brian well—Nick wondered if the commenters were now all dead—and they joked about Brian posting random shit to sell, asking what elementary school he robbed for this crap, lmfao. The objects were disturbing when viewed through the context of a man's pathetic and desperate offering: these benign artifacts now criminal, heartbreaking. This could be me, was what Nick thought, again and again, as he clicked through the same pictures. This was me. He thought of that night in his senior year when they were at Brian's house and after smoking a few blunts and snorting oxy someone had the idea to bake cookies, and then Nick had woken up to the smell of burned chocolate and smoke, an alarm ringing, and he looked over from his spot on the couch to find Matt in a recliner passed out but the windows and the slider door and the oven door were all open, and Brian stood in the kitchen, coughing and unsteady, swinging a towel in the air to beat out the smoke, saying wake the fuck up already, help.

But, uh, just to confirm: Nick Rizzo felt fine?

Oh, sorry, yes. Correct. So very fine.

Who did he have for support?

There was no need for support. Matt Wilson was in rehab. Which Nick respected. Supposedly it was a rehab where the children of millionaires rode horses.

Buford was busy. Which was a good thing. You wanted a man in business to be busy. And anyway Nick himself was busy, plenty of his own work, such as preparing to present horrible news to a board of investors.

What happened?

He planned to vacuum the couch, he was standing with the cushion in his hand, and he could not have known it was there. Someone must have left it during the party. Light slanted through the window and split the blocks of shadows. Smoke rose from a candle on the table. How could he have known? A wooden quiet clung to all. He stared down into the square beneath the couch cushion, where he found an abused and blackened spoon.

29

He located his hands. And, beneath his hands, his knees. Walls, ceiling, a pitiful fan. On the couch with a belt around his arm. By definition he knew it could not be yesterday. He stared at the television, mouth open, not knowing what to watch.

—

Dust rose off the arroyo into the mineral sky.

—

He discovered himself struggling to stay upright. In the kitchen, sliding, his back on the fridge. Outside Home Depot, against the fence, his fingers stuck in the chain-link. Down a window at the Chevron. Against a stucco column at Burger King. Walls, doors. It was as if he arrived late to his own demise. There was a sensation after he shot up, a sensation easier to miss by the minute, when he felt satisfied enough to forget who he was, what he said he would do, all he had not done. All else was the dope sick: about to puke, no end of snot, swirls of vision, feet crossed, his nulled words fastened with gauze. He did not want to die, but he did not know why he was still living. These facts conspired to prove he was still whoever.

—

The soundwave mountains halted.

—

There was a woman with a shaved head kneeling next to the candles. Nick was spilled, sweating, across the couch. Who was she? Kenny stood behind her, eyes closed, pulling up his pants. She chased with a straw the vapor off a hopeful square of foil.

—

A single desert willow, specked with white petals.

—

Then she was next to him on the couch, moving her hand through his hair. Her hand slid curiously, pausing, pinching. He noticed the distinct features of her touch—her palm, her finger knuckles, her uneven nails at the edge of a strand. He followed her hand with his own, discovering worrisome bumps. Bruises? Cold despondencies of bone. Tumors? To the touch he thought his hair thinner by the second. Impossible: his head was a mystery to his hand.

—

Brought to you by—a phrase that belled from the television, a phrase he found consoling, an attempt to explain the origin of the objects that pulled at his heart.

30

Memory was another surface across which he slid. Arriving, stoned, to his own childhood. Here was his mother, in commanding Sunday hurry. She had her hair down and wore her top-drawer pearls. Late for church. Every week. He noticed the beauty of their home sounds when in a rush. All the televisions, boisterous, at the same alarming volumes. Steam rising from the stove. His father, in his underwear and button-down, pacing around the couch with his slacks in one hand, lecturing across the ironing board. Doors opened, doors closed. Heels on tiles. The hinges of cabinets and slides of drawers. These were the sounds that meant they were a family. His mother, in the microwave window, revisiting her eyelashes. Her voice on Sundays its own revelation.

—

An unfinished freeway ramp, the concrete in the sky, leveled off to a dirt lot with a dozen backhoes left from the workday, the yellow machine arms raised.

—

Church and Harkins. These were the institutions that belonged to his mother. God, movies. Every Tuesday when she got off work they drove to the theater at the mall. Not kid movies, but her picks. "This is ours," she'd say, handing him the ticket, as they walked across the purple carpet colored with hideous swirls into the smells of liquid butter and arcade dust. Their usual: two large Cokes, refillable popcorn, Junior Mints, an Almond Joy they shared. Never more than a dozen people in the theater, exclusively the very old and the very young. Shuffling across the aisle for the middle seats. He could not remember a single scene from a movie they had watched, not one title, not even a comment his mother made. All he remembered was his mother's laugh. A rich eruption of sound, half-surprised at the force of itself. Her laugh filled the empty seats. It was then, only then, he understood his mother as separate from him, a bronze stranger. She did not try to muffle the sound with a hand but instead opened herself to the noise, her shoulders low and her chin high—here, his mother, in the light from the screen, convicted. It was how he imagined her even now as an adult, a modest redhead with a pointed nose, her face upturned in wonder.

—

Dry eyes in the petrified night.

—

"Hi, you've reached the voicemail of Allegra Constantino, owner of Arizona CBD Infusions, the top-rated company for oils, lotions, and gummies for you and your pets. Please leave a message with the reason for your call, and I'll be sure to reach out as soon as the universe allows. Namaste." It was his mother's voicemail again. He had not left a message. He had not left a message because he was scared for what it would mean if she still did not call back. Remarried, his mother was now, living in a hippie shack up north, running her own CBD business. She had survived cancer. She was fearless, busy, selfish, tough to reach. Without exception she texted near his birthday, messaged on Facebook, tagged him in old photos where he did not recognize himself—but she had not answered any of his calls.

—

At the Chevron each gas pump had a screen at its center, and the rows of screens tangled in a chorus, the recorded voices clashing through the same sentence.

—

His father, still underwater. A bottom-dwelling breaststroke in the apartment pool. Rolling ovals of light and limb across the crystal surface. Everyone watching at the edges. More than a dozen dripping boys, some with mouths open, all learning what it was like to be wrong. A bet had been placed. How long could Rizzo hold his breath? Up and back, up and back. Five bucks said no way. Even Nick had had his doubts as he collected the money from the kids. ("After we win, ask who wants to go double or nothing. Act skeptical. Drive it up." His father rubbed his nose while he spoke. "An easy fifty bucks for us. How about we do a nice Sunday dinner to celebrate? Me, you, your mother?") And there his father went, through the impossible, transformed beneath the surface of the water with a smooth roll to kick off from the pool wall. And the cheers when his father broke through the water a winner. Nick had felt himself yelling with the other kids, unable to distinguish the sound of his voice. "Double or nothing. Who's in? Double or nothing." His father, panting through his grin.

But then, from a door above, in a tank top and boxers, the father of Scottie Mingus. "Hey, Rizzo! Hey! You're stealing more of my money, by way of my son, when you already owe me two grand?" Shouts, curses, threats. Rizzo with the double bird. Mingus running barefoot down to the pool, grabbing the skimmer from the wall, wielding the blue rod like a lance, stabbing the water.

The kids chanting: "Kill Rizzo, kill Rizzo!" The bet shifting. "Five bucks on Mingus," someone yelled. "Five bucks on Mingus." And Nick, entirely still, watching as his invincible father splashed away from the skimmer.

—

Hours trembled from the new black road.

—

He liked to watch her walk with her shoes off. This was what she now did, on the landing outside the apartment: barefoot, arms out. Her name was Bri and she had cut a fentanyl patch with a steak knife, pinching out the substance that she then collected on a nailhead. Now she tried to place the heel of one foot exactly in front of the other's toes. She wobbled, tilted, faltered. It was like she slipped across the stones of a shallow river. Strands of her blond hair were stuck with sweat across her forehead. "God," she said. She was next to him, exhaling smoke. "It's hot as fucking balls."

—

A turkey vulture claimed a parking spot, squawking at a mess of carrion.

—

To wake to the sound of prerecorded applause. The television played an immortal game show. He was aware of having a wall behind his head, of becoming a seated witness to time. He thought of Bri's bare feet on the landing while he stared at the bean-shaped bag of dope on the table. The black rocks embedded in the walkway, filling holes. Boiling substance on the spoon, and the liquid-filled syringe, and the magnificent needle. He imagined her feet on the holes of the dated phone, and the voice of his shrunken father, rising from the bubbled substance, locked in orange, all alone.

—

"It's called buttfuck Egypt," someone said.

—

How many days? Lighting a cigarette in the pre-day dark. The delightful hurt of chewing ice cubes. How long? Maybe a week. Maybe a month. People hustling out of the parking garage, blinking through sunset. Darkness. The heat pushed through as daylight cut across the asphalt. Squinting while he smiled. He was slipping into perceptions. Blackened coins, gold bullets. The slot machine spin of the scroll. How long had he been lost?

—

On the wind the smell of gasoline.

—

The faded timeshare in Cabo. His father bragged to his mother that he'd gotten it for a steal, and to the flight attendant, and to the guy with a goatee across the aisle on the plane. The smack of light when Rizzo had pushed up the plastic cover on the window. His mother, shocked awake. The wind-shook sea, the white sand of the dunes. Children on bicycles outside the airport. The children, Nick's age, carrying pallets of gum packets. His mother, in a white floppy hat, tapping a sandal, while his father said that their bags would show up by the end of the day. Crammed in a cab down poorly paved streets. The cot at the foot of their bed that was supposed to be for him—but his mother, where she slept. Too afraid of the ocean, the hard waves pounding the green rocks. Too afraid of the pool at the complex, all the people, jumping and splashing. Too afraid the drinks contained alcohol, or that the water might be tainted, so he made his father take a test swig.

"Only for you," his father said. "You can't enjoy anything." His father struggled to light a cigar. "Who can blame you with a mother like that?" Puffing, puffing. Holding it out still unlit: "No matter what happens, I want you to know I love you, okay. Do you know that? You know that. I love you more than any goddamn thing in the world. You know that, right."

Pushed into the deep end of the pool by a stranger. An accident. It was the surprise of the fall that made him initially relent. Soon he became aware of the air all gone, the change in gravity, in weight—then he kicked and kicked. He could not remember why, but he knew he wanted to live.

At the airport, rushing to make an earlier flight, he had asked his mother if he could still love his father. His mother had crushed his hand, pulling him across the tarmac to board the plane. Once in her seat she had searched her purse for a loose stick of gum. Of course he could still love his father, his mother had said, but that did not mean, she continued, chewing hard, that he had to talk to his father ever again.

31

Buford Bellum, in a sweater that looked ready to unravel, said he was performing a wellness check. In the doorway Nick flinched from the daylight. It was colder than expected, the air hit him in the chest. "It's Christmas." Buford announced this as if Nick were to blame for the holiday.

"Christmas," Nick said.

They were on the couch, staring at the television. All the sadness now crashed across Nick's shoulders. He had his elbows on his knees, he was prepared to cry for the next decade. He was officially alive in the world he wrecked. The skin of his face felt twisted, he could not sit up straight.

"I met someone at the Taco Bell conference," Buford was saying. "Marla Sampson. She had an accent that was unmistakably Dutch. Said she owned a series of clinics that treated depression with psilocybin. She invited me to come to Amsterdam with her, effectively immediately. We connected on various profiles, she flew me first class. I took approximately two ounces of mushrooms during my stay. My ego was annihilated and then reconstituted into a malleable substance. I woke up and found Marla Sampson gone. Did she even exist, I wondered. It was easy to confirm that she did exist, Nick, because she had left not just with my wallet, but also with my laptop and cell phone. She knew all of my passwords."

"Oh." Nick was staring at his misshapen reflection in the corner of the flat-screen.

"She told me the last great secret each individual holds," Buford said, "is his or her password. And I believed her, Nick. And I still believe her. She said if we were to be truly open and honest with each other we needed to reset our passwords together and I could not have agreed more, Nick. So I've been wiped out. The feds are saying Russian. Which makes sense. Vikar Romanski—he was the friend who bought my Filiberto's franchise—wants to kill me. If I wasn't able to flip your house, I would have already thrown myself off a parking garage." A long pause followed. "Quick question for you," pointing to the corner of the room. "Who's that?"

That was Kenny, who was in a rocking chair with his eyes closed. Nick did not remember owning a rocking chair. But there Kenny was, wrapped in a fraying afghan, swaying. The gray light of the room showed the fading edges of his colored tattoos. Rigs and tinfoil were scattered across the table.

"Just to confirm." Nick's expression had not changed, he was still focused on his reflection. "My house is gone."

Buford put his hand on Nick's shoulder. "We needed the capital."

32

At the peak of Mummy Mountain was Buford Bellum's home. It was a triumph of stucco: an austere series of windows wrapped around six thousand square feet, two shedding palm trees in white Christmas lights framed the metal door. In the courtyard of the house, under the uneven shadows cast by the stacked roofs, there was a travertine fountain, the sound of the falling water frightening in its solitude.

They walked through an archway. "We're currently in a no-key situation," Buford said. He pointed to a box in a corner filled with gold locks and door handles. "The bank wants to foreclose? Well, I paid for those locks." Buford pointed at his chest while he said this. "Those locks are mine."

A chandelier, on the floor tiles, in the rounded entryway. Each exposed surface flawlessly smooth. White squares left by removed objects. Marble columns. Pedestals. Empty built-ins. A long hall, ending in shadow, with a rolled rug at its center. There was a formal dining area unoccupied except for an industrial butcher block. In the kitchen the ceiling towered above the painful shine of the countertops, the back of the house looked out on an edgeless pool. Nick in the kitchen, impressed and envious, next to the display of Talavera plates.

An armoire, a flat-screen. Two beds, both queen-sized, with purple velvet comforters, bulging pillows. Maroon carpet. A framed canvas streaked with shades of blue. Pile of rags, starchy, paint-smeared. Gilded lamps with patterned shades. A cheap standing fan, unplugged. The walls were exceedingly white. A partly opened window to Camelback Mountain. Stars above the hazy rock. It was as if life in the house had not yet begun.

33

There is a state of pain that eradicates all thought. Nick Rizzo was reminded of this, briefly, during his detox. He was pounding, crying, coughing. He was on the floor, on his back, alone. When he experienced this pain, he also experienced time, the mile of a second. Shredding, he knew, his stomach. Brilliant cracks inside his skull. He was aware of twitching, beating knees. Breathe, he told himself. Breathe.

He wanted to stand but his legs preferred otherwise. He was between the beds, on the carpet, half lit. It was the orange hour. He felt his ribs twist. Even he was surprised by how determined his body was to live.

34

He was a full ten days. Did not remember much except for Buford. Somehow, a friend. What had he done to deserve a friend?

He had been in the sheets, covered in his own shit. He fell across the shower tiles. Now felt a stinging embarrassment at the idea of being exposed without fully inhabiting his body. Buford helped. He brought water, buckets. Buford cleaned the buckets and brought more water. He did the laundry, he forgave the incident with the carpet. He seemed not merely tolerant but unfazed, as if this was just the most recent instance of someone wasting away.

Buford was in the room with a fireplace. The room was missing the other objects that defined it. No waiting room art, no portraits nor pottery. The open windows brought in the desert morning. It was January, new year. What had changed? Buford was in a wingback, dressed for sleep, staring out at the pool as if expecting the water to evaporate.

"Thank you," Nick said. He leaned against the wall, pale, thin. "Seriously." He took a breath.

Buford said, "I think I have something for us."

35

The camera ascends the amalgamated stone. The building is the color of the mountains behind it: green-swept, prairie style. Falling dust. Inside the house, a man in a suit is spread across a butcher block. It's unclear if he's dead or sleeping—that will be answered soon, it's why everyone is here: we're streaming live—but what's important is that he remains still.

—

To market is to confuse. It is done through juxtaposition, repetition, syllogisms, until the salvation of the South American rain forests can be found for a limited time in this table of solid hazelnut. The goal is to monetize anticipation, even dread.

—

It takes a moment for all else in the room to settle into place. Behind the man, above the fireplace, there's a wall-length canvas bearing a single color. There's a marble bar, candles placed along perfect surfaces. Tall windows, spotless, brandishing the stone vista before the pool that spills into the night. An unswayable chandelier drops above the body. The lights reflect in the floor tiles. To the room there's an inviting shine. Yes, around the body, all glows.

—

To market is not merely to sell. To market is to generate a system in which any form of transaction, including a sale, can occur. Therefore, the market is a liberated world, an atmosphere of relentless exchange, where one finds it impossible to conceive of the opposite of a transaction.

—

A man with a white beard enters the frame. He has rings, cufflinks, a gold watch. An introduction follows. Buford Bellum, a desert philanthropist, entrepreneur, one half of the mind behind what it is to follow, the event branded as a fundraising spectacle for Mass Survivors. He reminds viewers of the current crisis.

—

When survival becomes greed, when hope is exchanged for hunger. Kindness is exploited until only cynicism is rational. Remember: we are our context. Our context is determined by the invisible borders of the market.

—

Here is where expectations are set, the script run through. All from Buford. It is unfortunately true that everyone we know will die, and so on. However, that does not mean we should settle for an unjust death. Last year, there were more than three hundred mass shootings. Experts predict that by the year 2030, we will average four mass shootings per day. Soon every family will know someone affected, and yet our current treatment of survivors falls behind that of the weaponry used in the shootings. Just as we have seen our communities deploy a holistic treatment for those struggling with addiction, so too must we begin to think about our children and siblings and parents as they find themselves under fire in schools and churches and malls. A percent of what is raised today will go toward the Mass Survival Foundation, a nonprofit committed to assisting with the costs of medical and emotional treatment.

—

If anything can be deployed to market, then to market might mean anything.

—

Now without further ado: the man, on the butcher block, prepared to join a lineage of magicians and stunt artists and traveling circus strongmen. His current state has been achieved through a medically supervised intravenous overdose. He is stoned into oblivion. Wrinkled, sallow. He is terrifying in his stillness. He is concluding the greatest wait.

—

A nurse enters the frame. He's a skinny tattooed man who confirms that Nick Rizzo is not among the living. To prove it he lifts up the arms of Nick, which immediately drop. He pulls Nick up by his blazer, allows him to fall back. The nurse retrieves a makeup mirror from his pocket, breathes on the glass, and then shows the splotches of fog to the camera: this is what life looks like. Then he holds the mirror an inch or so from Nick Rizzo's mouth and turns the glass back to the camera: nothing. The nurse produces a bottle of nasal spray. Here is the moment we've been waiting for—will he survive?

—

Family is a threat to the market. Hence why the market targets the family.

—

Life as the smallest of acts. An eyelid twitch. Lashes flicker. We are so close that we will feel the eventual breath. He's staring upward now, his face square and pale and stubbled, an expression between joy and anguish, as if he's returned from a fatal depth with a stolen jewel. He cries in silent tears.

—

It is impossible to escape the market through the use of its own devices. (This is an unfortunate but frequent mistake.) There is no salvation in reclamation. That which is reclaimed has been altered irreversibly. Consider instead: silence.

36

There was a small concern. Namely, death.

But Nick liked the idea of reducing himself to a single decision, a last act. Come back to life a rich man, or stay dead. What, exactly, was the alternative?

Buford sat on a cooler with the arms of a sweater tied around his neck. Nick was leaning against the far wall, smoking, staring through the open window.

"You're sure," Buford said.

"I feel like I have to," Nick said.

They stayed in the room without speaking. A hawk appeared over the ledge, swooped across the shallow end of the pool, disappeared.

If successful, Buford said, he could imagine a franchise. The depressed, the anxious, the traumatized—they arrive at a legitimate medical facility to be taken on a spiritual journey, a regulated death experience. Lazarus Centers: strip mall sites of modern worship. This was beyond the ego death of psychedelics. This was it, the real thing, a brief end of physical being. There was a global need to improve the efficiency of spiritual pursuits. "If I'm right," Buford said, "we can offer transcendence."

37

He heard the truck in the courtyard an hour later than expected. Nick, next to the fountain, cigarette in his mouth, staring into the sun. The light shimmered the world.

"Please tell me you have limes," Kenny yelled. The engine off, the hot gravel bouncing on the axle. He walked to the bed and onloaded chairs, a table, pallets of tonic water. "I can only do Schweppes," he said. The bed of the truck was nearly filled with boxes: boxes of clothes, mostly, plus the rocking chair, a television.

"Why is all of my shit in your truck?" Nick opened the back door, found a mound of cables.

"Didn't Steve call you?"

"Who's Steve?"

"Steve's the man," Kenny said. He had opened a can of tonic water, lit a cigarette.

"Well my phone's fucked up. I probably missed it, I don't know. Why? What happened?"

"Basically he works for that management company. He kicked you out."

"How can he kick me out when I haven't been living there?"

"When someone falls off the roof at a party—"

"Why was anyone on the roof? And when was there a party?"

"Listen." Kenny took a few quick drags of his cigarette. He was in sweatpants and a flannel, his sunglasses were on the brim of his hat.

"I didn't come here to get angry about the past." He stared toward the house, then looked down at the stuff he had unloaded. "Shit. I parked too far away."

Later they were on the patio, on the wicker chairs next to the pool. On the table was a packed glass ashtray. Buford was in the kitchen, operating a blender. The sound buzzed through the windows.

"What a fucking shithole," Kenny said, staring at the pool. "With rich people it's all the same, man. Every house on this mountain, the same. People look at these mansions and get jealous? Think this shit is beautiful. Beautiful? All I see is corruption. That's it, man. Stinking corruption. This shit reeks! Standing on this mountain, looking at all of these mansions perched all high and mighty above the desert, like they're too good for the rest of us—*cor-rup-tion.* Swindlers. Inside traders. Goddamn pillagers. Probably never paid a dime in taxes. Probably funnel money from fake charities to pay for this shitty-ass pool. Probably fuck over little kids, the elderly, the retarded. Fuck over me, that's for sure. They get rich while I crawl around laying vinyl liner. Nice. How does it make sense that the harder the work is, the less you get paid for it? There's a fucking riddle for you. How come I can build this pool, but never afford one? Don't worry: that's rhetorical. I thought about this when I was driving up here. The higher I got on the mountain, the angrier I got. I don't know how to explain it. I just felt this sort of rage, looking at all of this bullshit. My mom and dad are rotting away in a trailer in the west valley, not two nickels to rub together. Meanwhile this asshole has an Olympic-sized pool in the desert, and I bet he's not even here half the year to use it. Yeah, the sight of all this money makes me want to fuck some shit up. Because this shit, this isn't real life, man. It's like one big porno. It's like we're all stuck in a porno, where it's obvious everything is fake, it's all a big performance, but we're all too desperate to acknowledge it, like we're so broke that we've got no choice but to play along and get dicked out from every possible angle. You know? You know. Yeah, when I was driving up here, I just got angrier and angrier until I felt sick. Seriously sick. I had to pull over. I thought I was going to puke." Reflections across the unblemished water—then ripples, when Kenny tossed his cigarette in the pool. "Hey, let me ask you something." Lighting another, inhaling hard. "How many times a day do you and that girl fuck? The one you and Matt used to double-team? What's her name. Elizabeth? Let me guess: she likes it in the ass. Ariel, she won't ever let me in her ass. We fuck three times a day. We're straight rabbits. I come quick but I go right again." Nodding. "Maybe we should do something. The three of us? Like a video. You know what I mean? Some bonus footage. Ha, ha. Or maybe just the two of us? Yeah, that might be good. Me, and your girl, and you—I don't know—watch?"

Buford arrived with a tray of drinks—tap water with ice cubes. "The blender died midway through," setting the tray on the table. He looked at both men as if he expected someone to stand.

After Buford had fallen asleep, it seemed only natural that they become remarkably stoned. The desire was somewhat sexual, Nick noticed, when Kenny showed him the foil ball.

Soon Nick was on his ass, in the garage. His head was back, his mouth open, he felt steady and true. The last thing he remembered that night was the space between the concrete and the garage door. He had insisted on cracking the door, a way in for the air.

In the morning he became aware first of his face. That is, one half of his face, which was flat on the ground. He stared at the gap beneath the garage door, noticed a pair of brown slippers. Buford, outside. Then he turned, gone.

38

"Well, hopefully this is still your number. It's me. You know, your father? Maybe you forgot what I sound like. Anyway, I'm about to be out. Released. Assuming you're not dead, I thought this might be of interest. The end of this week. Saturday. You know when Saturday is, right? The day after Friday? It would be nice if you could come get me. It would be nice if you could help me get back on my feet. Well then. I guess that's it. I'm a little nervous. Nothing big, but. Almost four years I've been in here. Anyway, I hope you're, you know. Eating. Exercising. We're going to exercise together when I get out. Push-ups, pull-ups. Good jogs. Can you at least call? We can coordinate pickup. Okay. Well. Love you. Yep. Hopefully this is still your number."

39

His phone charged only when he held the plug in the dock. Nick sat like this, on the floor, the phone flat across one hand, pressing the charger in place with a pinch. He stared at the locked screen of his phone for some time as if expecting the thing to explain itself. The screen was a piece of spiderwebbed glass.

What was today?

Saturday.

His father was somewhere, free.

40

Rizzo had left FCI prison six hours earlier, Nick was told. He checked bus stops, gas stations. What if he no longer recognized his father? Rizzo, anywhere, looking up from his spot on the curb. Nick would never know. If he left him, lost, did it mean their family would end?

Nick drove to the business park that once housed Rizzo's Firearms. A man with a shirt tied around his head knelt in the gravel, scratching behind the ears of a timid calico.

"Here's a question," Rizzo said, shading his eyes with one hand as Nick walked over. "Are you a fuckup? I'm sure you've wondered this. I'm sure you've asked yourself. You are not deprived of self-awareness, Nicholas. So? What's the answer?" Rizzo stood. The sky seemed to rise to make room for him. "You want to know how I got here? Let me tell you how I got here." He unraveled the shirt from his head. Sweat poured off him. "I waited at FCI for three hours. They gave me back my phone, but it was dead. So I walked across the street to the gas station, but the guy behind the counter said I couldn't charge my phone unless I bought something. I said, Why? I said, What law says that? He said he has the right. I asked him to show me where in the constitution it says some asshole with a gas station gets to play God. So then I was out near the pumps. I saw a truck with all of these window stickers for the Marines. Naturally I told the guy my situation, a veteran who was hard up, and I asked him for a ride here. In the car the guy asked me what I did in Desert Storm. I said I wasn't in Desert Storm, I was in Grenada.

He said what war was that again in a smartass way. I said, Don't worry
about what war it was, it was the Cold War. Then he said that wasn't a
real war. He said I served during peacetime. He said Grenada was the
greatest joke in all of American military history. Now mind you, this
was a large man. He was about six foot six, well over three hundred
pounds. This was not an ideal fight. But I looked over at the guy and I
go, Hey, buddy, first of all, I was also in Honduras and Nicaragua. I said,
Second of all, if you knew a goddamn thing about American military
history, you would know that there is no such thing as a peacetime.
Third of all, I said, if you knew anything about history in general you
would know that things get written in such a way as to keep people
from asking questions. And I said, Last of all pal you should worry less
about my time in Grenada, and more about the fact that your fat ass
is going to have a fucking heart attack any minute if you don't cool it
with those Fritos."

"What did he say?" Nick asked.

"He didn't say anything. He started to cry. He had a thyroid issue.
Started when he was on active duty. Said he'd been so depressed since
Iraq that he spent his days trying to eat himself to death. I felt awful.
This guy was crying so goddamn hard, Nick. Holy shit. I apologized and
apologized. He pulled over to the breakdown lane and made me get out.
But he pulled too close to the divider, so I couldn't open my door enough
to make it out. But he kept screaming: get out! get out! And I told him
I was trying, but the door kept whacking the concrete. I squeezed out,
but I was so focused on remembering this," lifting up a brown bag, "that
I forgot my phone in the guy's car. I tried to flag another ride while I
walked here. I had no idea what to do. Then I heard the cats in the old
spot. They remembered me. They nuzzled right up against my legs like
I'd never left. It was wonderful, Nick. I love those cats."

Rizzo pulled his arms through his shirt and then stared at his former
storefront, the tinted windows. Cats perched on the brick wall. He stuck

his hand out for the keys to the Eldorado. They walked toward the car without speaking, accompanied by the sound of the freeway traffic.

"Well, you've run this thing into hell," Rizzo said, opening the door. "When's the last time you vacuumed? Smells like a dog was fucking decapitated in here. The windows—how do you even see out of these. Christ. Are those cigarette burns? When's the last time you changed the oil? Please tell me you changed the oil. You've got coolant? Water?"

They were in the car, Rizzo had both hands on the wheel, and for a moment they were both still, and then Rizzo began to cry, brought his head against the wheel. There was a soft honk from the tap of his face. Nick did not know where to look, so he stared at his father, who had started to shake. Rizzo rose in his seat. He said, "I'm just so happy. I'm sorry. I've just never been so fucking happy."

—

"How stupid can you be," said Rizzo, when Nick tried to explain what happened to all the money. They were stopped at a light, in the merciless afternoon. The light was green but they did not move. Rizzo punched the wheel, then the dash. A car passed them in the right lane, the driver looking back. "You know what? Fuck it."

Rizzo reached in the back seat, tossed the heavy bag on Nick's lap.

"Open it. Come on. Open it already. You recognize that? That's my Ruger. I talked the guy in seizures into letting me have it back. You know how much that gun is worth? There's a pawn shop off Guadalupe. Fred Khan—that's who'll be behind the counter. He was a big supporter of me. Five hundred bucks. We're giving this guy a deal. I can't be seen on camera with the gun. My name can't be on the papers. But yours can. Got it? You do not walk out of there with less than five hundred bucks."

—

The pawnshop was an old white wood structure. American flags on the edges of the sagging awning. Not far from the edges of Indian land. Across the gravel Nick walked with a nervous hunch. He wanted to bury himself in the sand. Could he be a worse son? On the porch near the door stood a man in a surgical mask holding a leaf blower. There was a layer of dust over the porch planks. The man with the leaf blower scrolled on his phone. "My friend," said the man behind the glass partition. "What can I help you with, my friend?" Nick, glancing around. No windows. There were aisles of polished junk. Screens, gold chains, mounted rifles with sniper scopes. Behind the partition the man kept his phone flat on the counter, tapping while he spoke. He had spiked hair and was clean shaven and the face of his silver watch was bigger than his mouth. Again he said, "My friend."

—

Nick tried not to look at his father, but when he did he found what he expected: Rizzo, with his what-the-fuck expression, mouth open.

"Where's the rest of it?" Rizzo held up the cash. "Nicholas, where?"

Nick reclined his seat all the way back, folded his hands over his stomach, while outside the sky approached an early red.

Rizzo put his head on the wheel, shouting. "I thought you were the greatest gun dealer in the world! What the fuck happened? Did you even mention me? Did you say you were my son?"

"When I told him I couldn't do less than five hundred, he showed me his display of Rugers."

"Display."

Nick lit a cigarette, then rolled his window down. "He said it's a very popular gun for pawns. He said one hundred was fair. He lists all of his Rugers for two hundred and fifty. He wants good margins. It made sense."

"Go back in there and get the gun."

"What?"

"Are you deaf? Walk down that fucking road and go back in there and say sorry you changed your mind." He turned, hands on the wheel. "Yeah. I know a place in Peoria that'll give us six hundred for the Ruger. Fucking Fred. Yeah I know a place in Peoria run by a couple of Thai guys and I can guarantee you they don't have a single fucking Ruger there."

"But Dad what if he—"

"What did I say? Do you remember what I said? Go, I said."

—

The same man in the surgical mask, but now the leaf blower was flat on the porch. The bell on the door. "My friend, back already," said the man behind the partition. He held his phone away from his face. "What can I help you with now my friend?"

—

Night had started. A man stood in front of a Chevron, tapping the tire of a locked bike with his sneaker.

"What the hell took you so long?" Rizzo had his arms up, his seat belt on. "And where's the Ruger?"

"I need some Gatorade," Nick said. "Do you want anything?"

"What happened to the Ruger."

"It'll cost two-fifty. Now do you want a bottle of water or—"

"He's trying to sell the Ruger back to you for two hundred and fifty bucks."

"He said since I sold it outright, and since he showed me the display with every Ruger listed for—"

"Christ, Nicholas, did you use that fucking brain of yours to argue? Did you say no? Did you try to persuade?"

"I mean I said a lot of things Dad, but—"

"Talk him down to one fifty. He's made some quick cash for taking advantage of an idiot, my son, good for him. Walk back in there and tell him you'll give him one fifty for the gun final offer."

"I tried that already Dad."

"Fuck it. Fine. Whatever. Go back in there, pay whatever you need for the gun. Forget Peoria. We'll drive to Scottsdale and I'll sell the Ruger to this Black guy who runs a leather shop for eight hundred. Okay? Nicholas? Hello!"

Nick took off his seat belt. "Can I have the money, then?"

"Money for what."

"To buy the gun back."

"Use your money. I don't have any money, because you fucking lost it all!" He hit the wheel with the palm of his hand.

"Well this is what I have. It's a lot of ones. And they're stuck together." Nick held up the wad.

"I don't know what to say." Rizzo had his hands in his lap. "For the first time in my life, Nicholas, I am speechless. God bless you."

Nick, straight ahead: "I'm not going to do this thing with you where you just humiliate me and make me feel like an idiot because you have these insane requests."

"Fine. Where are you staying?"

"What?"

"Where?" Rizzo scratched his bald spot. "I need to sleep—so tell me where you've been living."

Nick put a finger to his mouth, closed his eyes, then pointed at Rizzo. "The thing about that is. See. Well."

"Am I a fucking homeless bum? Is that what you're trying to tell me?" Rizzo, looking forward. "Am I going to have to live in some rottweiler shitcan in El Mirage? Jesus Christ. I should've stayed in prison! Why did I think for a second that you would help me when all you've ever done is ruin my life? From the start. Ruin me. Selling my Ruger for practically nothing when I needed the money to live? Another drop in the well of the goddamn doom you've brought on me."

"I'm sorry, Dad. It's not that. You make it seem like I'm trying to—like it's my intention to—"

"Am I not invited to your place of residence?" Rizzo was looking at Nick now. "Are you so ashamed of me, your father, that I'm not allowed to sleep for a few nights in your drug den? Is that what it is? You're ashamed of me. You don't want to help me. After all I've done for you? You're too ashamed to bring me around your fucking rich buddy Buford Bellum?" He smacked Nick in the ear with his palm. Then he struck with the other hand.

"Don't hit me," covering his face with both arms. "Stop."

"You think that's hitting?" Rizzo punched through the gap between Nick's elbows. He leaned forward in his seat, punching. "This is hitting!"

"Dad—come on—stop—ouch. My eye!"

"That's how you hit! That's a real hit for you! *That* and *that* and *that*. Golden gloves your ass." Rizzo fell back in his seat, panting. "You want me to beg for your help? For basic human needs? Your father? You want to reduce me to a fucking beggar!"

"Okay, okay! Can I explain?"

"Christ, I'm out of breath," tapping his chest. "Could've used the money from the Ruger to put toward a fucking checkup!"

"I'm going to tell you the truth, Dad."

"What's the point? I mean, what is it?"

Nick told him about Buford, about Kenny, then said: "I need help. Like, I want to get my shit together, I want to stay sober."

"This is something I'm supposed to believe."

"What do you need to hear?"

"Let's get you into a rehab tonight then. If you're serious, I'm serious. I can make it happen. I met a guy in Florence whose sister runs a place. I've got the name. It's far. Yuma. But I can get you in tonight, no problem. Ricky was a big fan of what I was doing. His sister's name is Phyllis. They'll take you in for nothing."

———

They sat on the hood of the Eldorado, chewing. Few streetlights in the parking lot. A bundled figure far off pushed a clattering shopping cart. The occasional voice at the drive-through, then a car vanishing on the road. Rizzo leaned back against the windshield, a burger wrapper on his stomach. Nick hunched forward, shivering, beneath the unpolluted stars.

Rizzo held up his burger. "Mine's got bacon on it."

Nick, biting a nail: "What?"

"Bacon," Rizzo said. "Flame-grilled. Or broiled. Flame-broiled. Probably nuked in the microwave. I don't know. Bacon. If you want some."

"Do you know if this place does Suboxone? I'd like to be on something, if possible."

Rizzo, after a long sip from his cup: "Hey, let me see your eye, Nick. How's that eye looking?"

"It's fine. It's—ouch," flinching as Rizzo put his cup against his face. "That's cold."

"I hope you know the reason I get so angry is because I love you. I hope you know that."

"All right."

"All right?"

"What?"

"Well, it's just that you're about to go to rehab. We won't see each other for a while. We haven't seen each other for a while. Here I am, I'm communicating my love for you, and your last words are 'All right.'"

"They're not last words, Dad. This is rehab, not an execution."

"Let it be an execution, Nick. Let this be the end of the person you don't want to be."

—

What happened when they got to the facility should have been expected, Nick thought. Macbeth Recovery Homes. Inpatient, outpatient. A dying bulb flickered beneath the wood sign. The building itself was the same nondescript color as all the other desert stores. There were two main issues, said the woman who oversaw intake. Her hair was pulled back loose, she tucked her thumbs inside the wrists of her sweatshirt. Number one, they had arrived six hours past the cutoff for new arrivals. Number two, they were at capacity. She spared them the trouble and said no one within an hour drive could offer an open bed. The good news was that a spot could open tomorrow, if someone missed curfew. The wait list was purely symbolic. She got silence when she called down the sheet of numbers but was required to do it anyway. She told them to hang around tomorrow—they were twenty-first on the list—said she couldn't promise anything, but, who knows, you could always get lucky. His father had demanded Phyllis. "Can you just please go get Phyllis," he had said, but she was off tonight.

It was Rizzo's idea to sleep in the parking lot. Lights from passing traffic entered the shadowed interior of the car. Rizzo spread himself across the back seat. Nick was reclined, listening to his father breathe.

He thought of his father inside the facility earlier, the old Rizzo persistence. He had talked to multiple occupants and departers who wandered by the desk, reeled them in with cheerful greetings. "This is my son," his father had said, grabbing the back of Nick's neck. This is my son. At first Nick had been embarrassed, the adult whose dad took him to rehab as if it were his first day of school—but that embarrassment gave way to gratitude, and then pride.

My son, my son. I want you to meet my son.

41

Police Raid Paradise Valley Mansion After Live-Streamed Overdose
By Sarah Brickheart, CNN
Updated 11:05 PM EST, Sun February 20, 2018

Phoenix (CNN)—Scottsdale Police arrested Buford Bellum, a serial entrepreneur and venture capitalist, for charges ranging from investment advisor fraud, money laundering, reckless endangerment, illegal filming, and manslaughter.

According to a copy of the warrant obtained by CNN, authorities proceeded with a raid upon watching a live-streamed fatal overdose of forty-year-old Chandler resident Kenny Ghoul. The warrant states that Mr. Ghoul, a former adult film actor, was restrained to a hospital bed, where he received a fatal intravenous dose of fentanyl. In the video, Mr. Bellum can be seen failing to revive Mr. Ghoul during the live stream, attempting to use Narcan to no avail. Mr. Bellum is being held in the Estrella Prison without bail.

Before Mr. Ghoul received the fatal dose, Mr. Bellum claimed that all the funds raised during the event would go toward his newest charity, the Mass Survival Foundation, created to "support those who come out of a mass shooting alive and lost." Authorities are alleging Mr. Bellum's charity is just his most recent attempt to raise more money to cover debts accrued over years of failing business ventures. Mr. Bellum was already being monitored by the FBI for allegedly defrauding investors of millions of dollars for his businesses such as the Eiffel Tower Dealership, Hallelujah Landscaping, and PHX Home Hospice, among others.

CNN reached out to Twitter, Instagram, YouTube, and Facebook to learn how videos that seem to violate the terms and conditions of their platforms have been allowed to circulate for days. A spokesperson for Facebook suggested that it's possible their algorithms mistook the videos as a spinoff of the ALS Ice Bucket Challenge. ALS, also known as Lou Gehrig's Disease, is a disease of the nervous system with an unknown cause that can be fatal.

The live-streamed overdose of Mr. Ghoul, the first known live-streamed death of its kind, has **many worried** about the potential for similar cases, especially given the rise in live-streamed mass shootings. "We should not be surprised to see humans using digital technology to document death," said Dr. Fred Stamp, senior adjunct lecturer of Digital Media Studies at Southwest Oklahoma University. "Dying is the most human mystery," Dr. Stamp continued. "And the purpose of digital technology is to explain away all mysteries."

This story has been updated with additional developments Monday.

CNN's Debra Lahr contributed to this report.

42

.

He counted the days. One hundred and thirty-nine. That far from being someone else.

He studied the task between his hands, the material beneath his feet, the soft whistle of his breath—repeating the number. He missed heroin terrifically. But he got a number in its place. He could still joke. He worked to feel that every hour was a gift.

A staffing agency had distributed him to the assembly line at a clothing factory that was scheduled—if all went well—to shut down at Christmas. When he ate he smelled the stinging chemicals of the fabric dye on his summer arms, the starchy burn from the frightening logo press. He organized his life around a harmless malaise. This was the scorching month. Temperatures whipped down through sunset. On Saturdays he delivered food boxes. His days were slow, similar, right.

—

Near Maricopa Peak, his father climbed a ladder in the breaking sunrise. Rizzo, midway up, stared down at Arturo, who had a finger on a metal rung. It was an angled roof of pink tiles. Men tossed down chunks of rotted slate. "Okay. Andale." Arturo, offering an impatient smile. The pieces of tile fell like hail, sinking, cracking.

It was Rizzo's first roof. They had done yards, pools, full kitchen remodels, strict demolitions, but they had not done roofs. Now on top of the house, Rizzo crawled with exhausted worry: never leaving his knees, resigned with his hammer, witnessing the dust from the dropped tiles rise from the ground like fresh ash.

He was the slowest, the weakest. Too tender in demolitions. Too reckless in remodels. He was older by a tragic lifetime. He bent nails. He dropped wrenches. He was found, exposed, alone in his burning labrums.

There had been a friend: Miguel from Guatemala, a kid in his thirties obsessed with the New York Giants. He had a buzzed head, green eyes, he was lanky and hilarious. He had brought Rizzo in to help with his pranks—no one suspected Rizzo—which often involved hiding tools in lunch bags, or painting the ass of someone's jeans, but then one day there was no Miguel. Rizzo asked around. Everyone looked at him like he should know. Other people went missing but Rizzo said nothing.

Today he sat with his back against the house, in the shade, on the rocks, in line with the others, who were young and tanned and confident. He was in the middle, and everyone but him was talking, speaking across the valley of his silence, to share a water bottle's worth of tequila. Rizzo, the only one who did not speak Spanish. Even his white boss, Kyle, spoke Spanish. Kyle sat in his parked truck with Bible radio on, drinking with the windows down. During their breaks he made an appearance, smiling, ball-busting. Kyle, effeminate, with thin gelled hair, with a body soft from beer, younger than Rizzo by about a decade, and rich. To the next site Rizzo rode in the trembling bed of the pickup, throttled by the heat, clutching a damp towel to his skull, the tequila rising in his throat.

—

Rizzo and Nick lived together in a one-bedroom off Fifty-fifth and McDowell. They talked about dinner early in the morning. Rizzo brought home a cat with one eye, a fat orange stray that hid beneath the kitchen table for days, mewling. They named her Maria. Nick picked up a cheap record player that he found on the side of the road, and although the tone arm was missing, he used the machine for the built-in radio, playing baseball games he had no desire to watch but liked to hear because he enjoyed the sound of the spectators, the announcers narrating misses. They both still acted as if they were waiting to return to their home somewhere. It seemed impulsive to fully unpack. Together after work, they ate in front of the television, where nothing called up the labor of speech.

—

What remained, they both wondered separately. What was left?

—

Nick rode with Gavin Brickman to deliver food boxes. Retired engineer, recovering alcoholic, bitter Republican now in his early seventies, Gavin had never married, lived alone in a condo in Gilbert, where Nick imagined he ironed his khakis even on days when he had nowhere to go. He kept a fixed expression, his mouth tight. Never needed a phone for directions: every Saturday he drove to new places for deliveries as if he had been there, reluctantly, just yesterday.

Gavin was eager to lead the poor in prayer but refused to join hands. "I don't touch," he said, interrupting himself mid-incantation when a woman offered her fingers blistered from gout in the kitchen of her trailer. He was liberal with hand sanitizer. "Are you a Communist," he asked, once, back in the car, after he had seen Nick scratch the belly of a three-legged chihuahua. Gavin was the president of Saint Vincent, had been delivering food boxes throughout the valley for more than twenty years, had cut several personal checks to keep the pantry doors open. "Not that these people need food," he once told Nick. "They're all fat. They need vasectomies. They need their tubes tied. They need lobotomies." Gavin said this while reversing out of his parking spot at a motel with balconies of crumbling stucco. He was staring at Nick as he reversed—and he slammed the rear of his CRV into the concrete base of a streetlight. He stared at Nick while he screamed, ripping the shifter forward and back, the engine like his voice, shrieking.

Others were different. There was Dave Zhao, who had somehow been a software engineer, a screenwriter, and a stand-up comic, all before his current role as manager of the pantry. His wife, Sabrina, had lived more past lives than her husband: sold construction equipment, then IT software, opened a Whataburger, sold the Whataburger to open an In-N-Out, then opened a Kansas City barbeque place in Mesa, which still ran today, though she was trying to be less hands on. And then there was Felicia Ryan, who seemed both satisfied and bemused by Nick's appearance at the pantry, satisfied enough at least to participate in harmless chatter, give him a light when needed. She was always here. Today, for instance: Felicia, overseeing the sorting process in the room with green walls and no chairs. Priests stood around a table, fumbling squashes. Felicia carried two stacked boxes of vegetables over. Nick asked if Elise ever came around. "Haven't seen her," Felicia said. "She's got a job, a boyfriend. Practically someone else now."

Her number was the same, though. They talked on the phone, briefly, she told him to come by or whatever. Her place in Tempe had a carport and a broken hot tub. He found them in the backyard, Elise and her boyfriend, each on a lawn chair holding a cocktail shaker. She had lost weight, muscle. There was a slight glaze to her eyes, a slowness in her speech. She was in a tank top and jean shorts. This was her one day off a week, she said. And she still had a few calls to make. She was a pharma rep, spent her days in the waiting rooms of doctors' offices, dressed like a lawyer, an overstuffed duffel at her feet. It was a smaller pharma company—they specialized in OCD medication—but the hope was to be bought out by GSK. Her boyfriend was in his residency, an aspiring cardiologist. He was a goateed man in swim trunks whose legs were too long for his body. He stared over the top of his sunglasses, chewing on the wooden tip of a drink umbrella.

"You look like that guy who died," he said. "From the commercial. With the dad."

"That's him," Elise said. "He died."

"You can't believe everything you see on TV," he said.

—

It was through his son that Rizzo got back in touch with Felicia. He was prepared to apologize, to monologue about his self-transformation, his belief in miracles—but Felicia made it all unnecessary, said she still felt bad for spitting on him. Then, because being reminded of that was not enough: "You look so old now." Rizzo had ignored it—what could he say? was he old, officially?—and instead took silent note that Felicia herself had aged: her hair had gone gray, she was thin not from fitness but lack of appetite, and she walked a little slower, talked a little less.

Every Wednesday night he went with Felicia and the son of her boyfriend for dinner at a place off Bethany Home Road called the Grand Avenue Bar. They had fallen into this routine without any shared acknowledgment. The inside of the bar looked like a hallway with chairs. In the winter the front door was propped open with a cinder block. The kitchen was a tiled room where a bar back made the turkey sandwiches, and on weekends a revolving cast of local bands played a form of country heavy on the electric guitar out here, everyone packed in to smoke and talk and dance. Nick never joined. Neither did Felicia's boyfriend, Earl. Wednesday night was when Earl shot pool. He owned a custom cue with a baby rattlesnake preserved in amber at the base—he showed this to Rizzo the one time they met—and he seemed somewhat grateful that Rizzo wanted to spend time with his son and Felicia while he went off to practice trick shots. Stan was the name of Earl's son. He was in his mid-thirties and autistic, he wore Iron Maiden T-shirts and thought Rizzo was the most fascinating person in North America.

"Okay, Stan," Felicia said tonight, after he fell from his stool—she had told him, several times, to quit leaning back on the legs of his stool—and now the man was on his back, crying ecstatically, and Rizzo was struggling to pull him up by his wrists. Felicia, watching, finished her beer. The bartender looked over with a mild curiosity as he poured tequila into a rocks glass.

There were times when Rizzo could not resist feeling pitiful—such was the case tonight: trailing a woman who once hated him and still had no interest in sex with him to a bar built for weekdays—but more often there was gratitude, a warmth in his face when he turned and saw only neon in the window.

—

It was Nick's idea that they should talk more. It seemed they talked the most, Nick said, only when they knew each other the least, after long separations. Yet here they were, living together, in silence, when they should have been talking. But talk about what, Rizzo wanted to know.

They were both on the couch, watching Nick switch channels, the moments splintering on the screen.

Rizzo continued: There's nothing to say to someone you see all the time. Why would we talk about what we both know? If we both know something, there's no reason to say it. Sometimes being polite meant pretending you did not know something when you did.

Nick guessed that what his father had described was in some sense the root of conversation, but he doubted they knew all the same things, father and son, and that was why he thought they should try. To talk, to know. Did his father agree? Silence. Nick looked from his reflection on the screen to his father, who, next to him on the couch, with his chin resting pensively on his hand, had already fallen asleep.

—

Why was love so hard to show?

—

The rehab in Yuma had been unremarkable, in line with expectation. After the abysmal detox had ended—the crippling soreness, the restless legs, the throbbing sinuses—he fell through the next twenty-five days in silence, despondently aware that he had nothing to look forward to, a pessimism confirmed by the month he lost in a halfway house listening to the same set of tattooed dumbasses from rehab dreaming aloud about how they would get laid or write a Pixar script or start other shitty rehabs of their own—but it was in the halfway house that he had volunteered at a food pantry. This was all he brought back to Phoenix with him on the boiling bus: sixty days clean, a duffel bag of wrinkled clothes, a childishly naive desire to volunteer.

The food distribution center was in the back of a church and had the word *saint* in its name but for an unexplained tax reason remained lawfully godless. Nick helped with the unloading and sorting and stacking of new deliveries because he believed in this work, the unseen preparation before the morning lines arrived, private, true. He once spent an entire afternoon ripping plastic bags from a dense roll. He stood above a steel table, pinched a corner of plastic to stretch the material out until the perforated line was visible, then tore the line with a press of his palm. The key was to stack the torn bags evenly so that they did not clump together.

Nick asked Gavin once if they could use paper bags instead, and Gavin said of course, but Nick would just need to cover the cost, which, by the way, was double the amount.

Outside trucks left pallets of dented food cans. Farmers dropped off pounds of ugly vegetables. Nick knew that what he did was hardly helpful. Unloading. Loading. Visiting a home with a box. Skim milk, brandless bread, cans of beans, pastas, nonperishables. But he felt of some slight use, carrying things up the stairs.

It was Gavin who led the unasked-for prayers. Nick loaded, carried, dropped off. No one spoke to him, no one bothered to play a role for his benefit.

Once he visited a home near the airport with dirt floors, no running water, a high fence of barbed wire. Takeoffs shook the foundation. Through the windows the turbines sounded like detonated bombs. Gavin checked off the items in the box on his clipboard. Nick was struck by the presence of a big-screen television, how electricity could course through a home with no running water, how a source of entertainment could hang above dirt floors. He knew this would be his priority, too. A television over floors.

Later that day, at a trailer park with a drained pool, Nick marveled at a woman who answered Gavin's questions with impressive disinterest. Nick carried the box inside, set it on the floor where she told him, and then, while Gavin began his unscripted and unapproved questioning—are you looking for a job? when did you last apply? why do you think you haven't heard back? where do you plan to apply next? (Her answers: "Yep. Yep. I don't know. I don't know.")—and while Gavin asked, she took from the cardboard box the pound of hamburger meat, dumped the whole cylinder of red beef on a skillet, sent up a flame. The meat turned gray as it cooked. From holes in the ceiling came the ring of wind chimes. The woman cooked as if Nick were not there, crumbling the beef with a wooden spoon. This was beautiful, he thought: to be invisible.

He found himself in this state more often. Like when he was alone in the storage closet, filling the shelves. He liked the clear weight of the cans. He kneeled, reached. He climbed the stepladder, obsessing over the alignment of the beans. He wanted colors, brands, all to make sense. It was here that he found himself thinking more of his prior life, New York. In the crowd on the train he had found a downcast comfort. Late when drunk riding the subway alone he had feared the presence of the seats, the windows with views of art-splashed tunnel walls, the rough speed that pushed his body back. There was no fear now in the room with the cans of food.

—

Miles north, the excavator was unmanned, parked beside the hole that would become a pool. In the hole were a dozen men. No one moved. In the dirt, on his knees, fighting for breath, Rizzo tried to explain to the group that he was okay, that this was nothing more than simple agita. Water fell on his head, blurring the world. He spat, shook, wiped, spat more. His hands were on the rocks now. More water fell. He looked up, dizzy. Genetics, emotions, he said, all mental. It was Arturo pouring the water. As soon as Rizzo lifted his head he thought he would fall again, the morning was that damaged: exploding through his skull. Kyle walked over, he was talking from the ledge. It was the tequila, and the goddamn sun, and the sausages he'd had last night for dinner—the acid, the alcohol, the summer. He needed some water, some shade, that was all. His tongue was uncompromising. He did not believe what he was saying but nevertheless forced himself upright. Everyone still stared. From what Rizzo could determine, even Kyle had an expression of concern. But Rizzo was fine. Stumbling, he retrieved his shovel and swung it down into a scatter of brush. The shovel could be a crutch. All returned to their expected roles as he worked the earth judiciously.

—

They were on the couch, in front of the television, watching an advertisement that involved a seagull and life insurance, when Nick asked his father how work was. And don't just say good, Nick said, with a rehearsed cheeriness. Rizzo said work was okay. He had just gotten out of the shower and was already sweating.

Okay, Nick said. Great. He turned off the television and they both continued to look at the blank screen.

Nick missed when, years ago, just sober in the old house, they sat across from each other and talked as if the table existed only to hold up their speech. He had felt close to his father and closer to himself. This was what talk did, assured him of himself. He wanted to feel that again, the trust. He could not remember the things they had said to each other, in exact detail, but he knew with certainty the force with which they had said them. He missed this. He wanted this.

So, how was work, he asked again, his voice lower. But before Rizzo could answer, Nick noticed the mark on his father's elbow, a scrape. What happened there? Nothing, Rizzo said. Nothing? How was that nothing? It already looked infected: the ring at the edges, the bubbled pus. I fell, Rizzo said. Fell? Why? There's no big why, Rizzo said. He tripped over his own boots, he said, a mistake, a nothing. Was it because of the heat? No. Did he feel okay, internally? Yes. When was the last time he had been to the doctor? He didn't need to go to the doctor. But when was the last time? Didn't matter. But he should go now, nevertheless, for a checkup. He wasn't getting any younger, and the work would not be any easier, and he should make sure everything—his heart, his stomach—was up for the demands of his labor. Okay. Okay? So would he? Go to the doctor? No. Because Nick would pay for it, if that was the concern. How would Nick pay for it? That was not the concern, Nick would figure it out, so why would Rizzo not just agree to go to the doctor for a quick checkup? Because he fucking said no! That's why! How many times had he been to the doctor? How many? And for what? To be told he did not need to go to the fucking doctor?

Rizzo grabbed the remote from Nick, turned the television back on. Enough with the questions, Rizzo said. Enough with the fucking talk! Talk. Right. A lot of good he'd gotten from talk! He did not need a doctor, just like he did not need a nagging fucking son! What he needed was some silence! Or would he have to go back to prison for that? Peace and fucking quiet?

Nick said nothing. There was the sound of Rizzo breathing from his mouth: phlegmy, rapid. It took some time for him to realize what was on the screen. Helicopter angle of an evacuation. Updates on a shooting in Santa Fe. Kids in a parking lot that cut through a plain of desert brush, jogging with their hands up. Rizzo watched this, breathing louder. The chyron: four confirmed dead, including shooter. Look at that, Rizzo said. I hope whoever gave that idiot a gun has to go to jail, too. Yeah, they should let me sit on the fucking jury. Here's a peer for you! They should send that guy to the fucking electric chair! That's what I wish they did to me. Better off. Forget prison. Prison wasn't the worst. The worst was having to come out of prison and have nothing—to be a felon living in this ass crack of town with his son who won't shut the fuck up! He had wanted to do good, remember? After the shooting, he wanted to change his life—but what good could he do? He was useless! He had been made useless! Rizzo threw the remote at the wall. He leaned on an elbow, panting.

The temp agency could get Rizzo something better, Nick said. He would make a call tomorrow, see what they needed to fill first.

Silence.

It wasn't the job, Rizzo said. He liked his job. He was fine. He had both elbows against the wall. He covered his face with his hands, breathing. He was sorry. He did not mean what he said. He felt he was waiting to die. That was all. This was what disturbed him most. That he had nothing beyond his own end.

—

Was this true? Rizzo, with nothing pending, but the fall of the curtain of his life? If so, why not rejoice?

—

The strange names of businesses. These were what Nick printed on the shirts at the factory, corporate operations. He fitted the heated shirt on the press, a machine that resembled a waffle maker, and then he lowered the top, steady in the steam. Aching noises from the machines. The exhausted ventilation, the veteran workers' conversations. When he unclamped the structure he found the name on the fabric, a name remarkable for its lack of correspondence to any object in the desert. Nextech, Biostart, Greenheart. Text formed of black blocks. What need did these businesses fill? Futrtouch, EMA, Simple Practice, Duda, Arcturus. Hieroglyphics of the new millennium. Did these names stand for something, indecipherable acronyms? Or had they risen as fully formed to their creators, who privileged sound over sense?

This morning Nick had called his contact at the temp agency, Melissa Osher, a former actress from LA who had once starred in a Snickers commercial—she had told Nick this when he mentioned the advertisement—before she moved back to Phoenix after her mother's second stroke. "Your dad's not a felon, right?" Melissa had asked. "Because as long as he's not a felon, we have options. Otherwise, it's construction." Nick said nothing while Melissa listed all the options for those with no federal criminal history.

—

It was Wednesday, so they were alone at the bar. Rizzo watched Stan hold his phone sideways and click the screen. Rizzo had a question for Felicia, called it out over the hunched head of Stan.

If she could travel anywhere, where would she go? Felicia looked at him and then down at her drink. Rizzo wanted to plan a trip together, he said. All three of them. What were her thoughts on the Petrified Forest? He had never been, but he heard there were purple cliffs and gold brush, swirling rings of unearthly colors. Maybe they could camp above the valley, wake in the dark to boil coffee and see the sun break through the dawn to hit the special rock.

"I'll be sixty next week," Felicia said, and then she said nothing for some time. She picked at the skin of her hands. "When I was twenty, I thought my life would be over by the time I was sixty, that I'd basically be the walking dead, nothing to look forward to, all desire dried up. But you know what? It's the exact opposite. I've got no real family. No job. I'm free. The money from selling the business is almost gone. I'll have to figure something out. At sixty, I'll have to scrape together a life. There's all this possibility. And it's terrifying, yeah. But it's because I'm free." She looked at him for the first time in what felt like years. "Isn't that beautiful?" she asked.

Was it? Because he was not sure, Rizzo agreed, and then shifted to other matters. But days later, while on a roof, on his knees, he returned to the idea. Free? Hammers struck like cosmic drums. He felt the collisions in his wrists, in the sides of his neck—a raucous pulse. He was aware of the work needed to breathe. He looked up from his hands at the brass day where smog clung to the roofs. Traffic, garages, suburb sounds. Toward the crash of the horizon the birds faded. In the distance, the Eiffel Tower Dealership. The cars seemed to be parked in the sky. Free? He was still thinking of what Felicia had said. On his knees he studied the spinning yard below, the cars parked against the curb at the base of driveways.

Kyle stood outside his truck talking to someone Rizzo did not know. They were smiling, all was fine. Kyle had an AR-15 against his stomach, showing off the gun, or attempting to. He was struggling to bring back the bolt, so he rested the gun against his torso and tugged with two hands. The gun became a limb reaching out of Kyle's stomach. Rizzo watched this for some time, then crawled toward the ladder; his chest still hurt, he wanted water, but on his way toward the edge of the roof something went wrong, his boot found only air and soon the same was true of his hands and his body commenced a slow rotation down that concluded on the concrete. No one heard his fall over the hammers.

Nick would not learn what happened for several hours. After work, at Chevron, he smacked his pack of cigarettes, yawning in the sun. Why would he have thought anything was wrong? On his way to the bus stop he heard his name. "Nick! Hey, Nick!" He was still on the sidewalk and did not recognize the person calling out. A convertible in a state of disrepair rolled toward him. Nick did not know whether he should be thrilled or terrified to see Matt Wilson at the wheel.

"I'm like you," Matt said. "Back from the abyss." He had the same thin face, bones clear, intimidating. "I'm on the way to Vegas," he said. "Just for the weekend. A last hoorah." Matt had fallen back into the expected cycle, but he was over this whole thing, chasing drugs, he wanted stability, so Vegas for a major blowout, and then come back to detox. "Splitting the cost of gas would be nice," Matt said. "Do you want to?"

It was a question that might have meant so much. Nick leaned against the door of the car, smoking. What occurred inside his head then, in the time between understanding and a response, was the same thought that came to his father in that drop to the earth: he was free.

"Nick?

"Hello?

"Hey. Nicholas . . .

"*Nick! Nico!*

"Jesus fucking Christ. Hey! Hello!

"Forget it. Just forget it. No point. Never was. Never will be. Why bother. Numbnuts over there asleep in a chair with the remote in his hand."

"Ah, shit. How long was I out?"

"Out, right."

"I was sleeping."

"That's very funny."

"It's been a day."

"Oh yeah? Wow. Huh. Long day? Well. Whew. Sorry about that. Yeah, so sorry to disturb your slumber there, *Mr. Sleeping fucking Beauty!* So sorry to wake you! But hey—you know something? Hey, maybe—if you're not too tired—you wouldn't mind telling me what the fuck is going on!"

"You have to relax, Dad. They were very clear about this. Surgery is a—"

"Surgery? Are you kidding me? Surgery? Get me out of here before they figure out where to send the bill. Come on. Hurry up. Toss me in that wheelchair and shove me down the stairs. How did I get here?

Please don't tell me it was an ambulance? How the hell am I supposed to pay for an ambulance?"

"It's the helicopter that's really going to cost us."

"The what."

"The helicopter, Dad."

"I'm sorry Nick it sounds like you keep saying the word *helicopter*. But I don't know why you would be using that word."

"The first ambulance took you to—"

"There were multiple you're saying. Ambulances? Ambuli? You're telling me several were involved."

"Dad, you were working on a house in Apache Junction. You fell off the roof. At first they thought it was just some broken bones and a concussion so the ambulance drove you to—I forget the name of the hospital."

"What does the name have to do with anything?"

"That's right: Dignity Health. Anyway, one of the nurses there noticed how high your blood pressure was, they did some scans, you have a blocked carotid artery. Like almost completely blocked. They weren't sure how you were even walking around, let alone climbing on roofs. They did the medevac helicopter to get you to HonorHealth for the emergency surgery."

"And you didn't stop them? You didn't think to say your father would prefer the scenic route?"

"I was still at work. I'd gotten a few calls from random numbers, but I never answer random numbers. They make me nervous."

"That's great. That's really wonderful. You spend your whole life looking at that screen waiting for something important to magically announce itself, and then when this consequential event occurs, you're too scared to answer the call."

"I get that you're angry, Dad. Trust me, I was angry too when I heard they couldn't land and had to fly back to Dignity—but it's a miracle you're alive right now. Truly."

"They couldn't land."

"HonorHealth had a lockdown drill happening. But the pilot wasn't told, so they were flying around HonorHealth, waiting for a signal to land, and eventually the pilot decided it was in your best interest to fly back."

"My best interest? If this guy wanted to do what was in my best interest he should've pushed me out of the helicopter."

"Honestly I'm surprised you're not in more pain. Four broken ribs. Four. One of the ribs was less than an inch away from puncturing your lung."

"Only I would get so lucky. Helicopters, ambulances, surgeries. I'll never get out from under this. It's over. This is worse than death. How will I work? The debt, the injuries. How will I afford to eat? I would be lucky to die. If the roof had only been a few feet higher. If there'd been some pickaxes on the ground where I fell. If the first ambulance had driven a little faster, sent a rib through my lung."

"Don't worry, Dad: you'll be done with the surgery in a few hours."

"What do you mean a few hours? I thought they did the surgery. I thought it was an emergency."

"It was—it is—an emergency, and they tried to, but there was an issue with the vascular surgeon. They found him passed out in the handicap stall. Drunk, stoned."

"So the surgery is still happening. There's no way out of it?"

"The new surgeon is prepping right now. I was hoping you wouldn't wake up before it. I didn't want you to get nervous."

"Okay."

"But I also wanted you to wake up. It's strange for me, being back in the hospital."

"Yeah."

"I came back while you were in prison. My friend overdosed one night. I saw him today. He was on his way to Vegas. Asked me if I wanted to go. Of course I wanted to, but I said no. I said I had to get home to see my father. I didn't know you were hurt yet. But I meant what I said. If I hadn't thought you were home, if I didn't have you in my life, I would've gone."

"Hey, Nick."

"There was this moment when the nurse was telling me what it will look like after your surgery. The therapy, the prescriptions. And there was this moment when I thought to myself—and I'm just being honest, Dad—but there was this moment when I thought, Can I do this? Can I take care of you? Can I make sure you take your pain meds? What if I slip up? What if you get addicted? What then? But then I thought of telling Matt no. That's how I know I can do it, Dad. Take care of you. That's how I know."

"Hey, Nick? They have to put me under for the surgery, right? Anesthesia?"

"Well yeah, I mean it's a carotid artery they have to cut open your neck and then—"

"Nick, I can't, okay? I can't."

"But Dad all they do is slice your neck—"

"What if I don't wake up? What then? This happens. People who are sick they die in surgery. They never wake up."

"Dad, if you're that worried about dying, you should be grateful for the surgery."

"I'm not worried about dying, Nick, I'm worried about being killed. I'm worried about some anesthesiologist who had an extra shot of espresso giving the gas a crank. I'm worried about the surgeon sneezing while he's got a scalpel in my neck. I'm worried about some meth-head nurse fucking up my IV and sending an oxygen bubble into my brain. I'm awake, Nick. I want to stay awake."

"You're going to be fine, Dad."

"All my life I've lost. All my life I've fucked up. You, your mother, my parents, my uncle Gio, those kids at the school—it didn't matter. When people think of David Rizzo, they think of a loser, and that's fine, that's fine and okay, as long as I get to live."

"No one thinks that."

"What will I see?"

"Nothing, Dad."

"Major? Do you think I'll see my dog, Major? And my parents—will my parents recognize me? I've always wondered this. When you die, wherever your soul goes, if it takes on the best version of yourself, then how will anyone recognize you? If my parents are young, I won't recognize them. I'll be dead and alone."

"You're going to get surgery on your carotid artery. They'll clean out the artery. You'll wake up from the anesthesia."

"What will I see? Seriously Nick now is the time don't hold back just tell me the truth. When I die, what will I see?"

"Nothing Dad. Nothing. You're not going to die. You'll see me, and then you'll see the Eldorado, and then we'll be home."

ACKNOWLEDGMENTS

To Rebekah Jett, dream editor—a thousand thanks. To Michael Mungiello—a dear thanks. Also a major thank-you to Kathy Belden and everyone at Scribner.

Thank you to my teachers and heroes: Dana, George, Jenny, Jon, Mary, Nana.

Thank you to friends and encouragers: Jackson, Alexandra, Aprea, Walker, Bud, Bible, Jimmy.

To my family—for the love, thank you.

And thank you to Kelley, my love.

Alexander Sammartino lives in Brooklyn. He received his MFA from Syracuse University.